When Sirens Scream

Robert E. Rubinstein

DODD, MEAD & COMPANY • NEW YORK

All characters and places in this book are fictitious, and any resemblance to actual persons living or dead or to existing places is purely coincidental.

1   2   3   4   5   6   7   8   9   10

Library of Congress Cataloging in Publication Data

Rubinstein, Robert E
When sirens scream.

SUMMARY: A 16-year-old boy tries to arrive at a
decision—to side with his father who is investigating
the safety of the town's nuclear plant after an alarming
"accident" or with the townspeople who need the jobs and
tax money provided by the plant.
[1. Atomic power plants—Fiction.   2. Fathers and sons
—Fiction]   I. Title.
PZ7.R83135Wg   [Fic]   80-2788
ISBN 0-396-07937-7   AACR1

ACKNOWLEDGMENTS

Many thanks to my special readers: Linda Brodie, Marion Bennison, Marilyn Kays, and Peggy Rubinstein, and also to Linda Erz and Laura Mason. For his expert technical advice: Dr. David Clark, Ph.D. in Biology, University of Oregon.

"The future has no cure for the past."
—*Anonymous*

1

"You don't have to go so soon. I mean—well, we left school so late—and we've hardly even had a chance to be together, by ourselves."

Ned Turner had already reached the front door. He turned to look at Kathy. "Yeah," he said, "I'd like to stay for a while longer, but Mom would be a little up-tight. She needs me at home soon."

Kathy stood there in her socks, ten feet away from Ned. Strands of her brunette hair hung down over her left eye. She shifted her slim, petite, sixteen-year-old body from one foot to the other. "You could stay. It'll be lonely without you here—until Dad or Mom finally comes home."

Ned smiled. "And what should I tell my mother?"

"Nothing." She shuffled her feet back and forth, and clasped her hands behind her back. "Tell her that I kidnapped you."

Ned continued smiling. At that moment she looked like a young girl who knew she had said something she shouldn't have.

"My folks wouldn't mind. Dad likes to see you. He thinks you're his never-born son or something. OK?"

He walked over to her and placed his hands on her shoulders. He gently pulled her close to him. "I really don't think it's a good idea. Besides, my mom does expect me home by five. I have to watch George while she makes dinner. That gives me—as of now, ma'am—just forty-five minutes, and it takes nearly thirty minutes or so to walk from here."

Ned kissed her lightly on the lips. He released her and walked quickly to the door. Turning the handle, he pulled the door open.

The blasting sound of sirens suddenly shrieked at him.

Their piercing sound shot down the streets of Wilkenton, shot through house walls and people's ears. The sounds shot through the people themselves, rattling their bodies.

For several seconds, Ned froze with the door open. Then he seemed to come back to life. He quickly shut the door and backed inside the house until he reached Kathy's side.

Kathy gave him a half-enthusiastic, half-worried smile. "Guess you stay for a while after all."

"Guess so—at least for the standard fifteen- or twenty-minute alert. Aren't we the lucky town to have those things around to shriek at us, to keep us on our nuclear toes? The federal government really did it when it decided by itself to have nuclear plants in rural areas set up siren systems. Just like trained mice, we're all supposed to come in from the 'field' back to our home-bases whenever that thing goes off for a test. Then we wait around to receive further instructions. Really weird!"

"I just want you to know, Ned Turner, that *I* did *not* tell them to start those sirens shrieking just to keep you here a little longer." She tried to sound light and cheerful.

"You didn't? That's what you say, miss. But I know the pull you have with those guys in the nuclear plant up there. You just give them a flash of your smile, a sweep of your hair, and shake your body, and they set those sirens wailing for you. I know."

Kathy's smile stayed for a moment longer and then disappeared.

The long, sharp siren blasts continued.

Kathy shivered in Ned's arms.

Neither one of them said a word for some minutes. They just felt the siren blasts together.

Ned wrapped his arms more tightly around Kathy. He led her over to the couch where they both sat down.

"What's the matter? Why are you shivering so much? You cold?"

Kathy shook her head. "Those sirens make me shake. Whenever I hear them it makes me feel like my whole body is coming unglued or something."

"Hey! Come on, now! You've lived here—for what?—over two years? How many times now have you heard those sirens blast out like that? Fifteen, twenty times? Nearly once a month, maybe? It's only a test, another safety precaution. That's all."

Off in the distance, they could hear the prerecorded voice over one of the mobile bullhorns that moved up and down the streets of the town once the sirens stopped their screaming. "This is an alert—an alert. Please listen to your radios for further information. This is an alert—" The same words were repeated over and over—and faded—as the bullhorn passed the house and on down the street.

Ned gave a little laugh. "Even those words haven't changed in the two years or so since the government started those sirens screaming at us because of that nuclear plant. You'd think they could come up with a more creative announcement or something."

He could still feel the shivers running through Kathy's body. "Hey! You're as bad as my little brother George—only he hides under the bed every time that thing goes off. Look, you know it's a test—a way of keeping us prepared in case anything really bad should ever happen at the nuclear plant. And nothing ever has. It's like the fire drills we have to have every month at school. Just a test so we know what to do in case something like a fire happens."

"I know it's a test." She said the words very softly. "But how do we know when it's *not* a test? One of these times it could be the real thing."

Stroking her hair, he lowered his head and kissed her on the back of the neck. "If it's ever not a test, they'll tell us— we'll know. But that's not going to happen, so stop worrying. They have scientists up at the plant—top engineers—federal regulations. Besides those people, they have all kinds of safety systems, and backup safety systems. The chances are that nothing's going to ever really happen. They're so safety-conscious that they keep having those sirens go off—just to keep us awake. I think they're really afraid people take too many naps."

"But when they do go off like that, when I hear that heavy voice move up and down the streets, I think of my father.

He's up there. If anything should happen, what would happen to him?"

"Nothing's going to happen, OK? I know you worry, but it's OK. Those sirens going off like that are enough to scare anyone. At least, if there's a fire, you can see it—smoke and flames. But with radiation from a nuclear accident, I don't know what you could tell. It would be sort of invisible, I guess. But nothing's ever happened up there—has it?"

Kathy didn't answer immediately. "My father said there have been a few things that have happened. A few men got too close to some radioactive stuff. Another got some contaminated water on his clothes, and they wouldn't let him work near nuclear materials anymore."

For a moment, Ned had nothing to say. "But no one heard about any of that, so I guess it wasn't any big deal."

"No. They were OK. One got a little sick or something, and was out for a few days, my father said, but he was back at the plant and doing all right after that."

Ned smiled. "So? What's to worry about?"

She sighed and hugged him.

Ned gently stood up, lifting her to her feet also. They walked over to the living room window and looked out.

No one—nothing—moved on the street. Then an orange-striped cat ran screeching across the street and dove into a neighbor's hedge. Shortly after that, a barking dachshund, smaller than the cat, hurriedly waddled across the street in hot, slow pursuit of the orange-striped cat.

They both laughed as that funny-looking dachshund dove headfirst into the hedge and got stuck there.

The tension flowed out of Kathy's body. The fleeing cat

15

and the waddling, rushing dachshund seemed to say everything was still all right out there. Nothing had happened to their world.

"Look at that dachshund go! Do you think it's a boy dachshund chasing a girl cat, or the other way around?" Ned held her close to him.

"Who cares!" she laughed. "It's just good to see."

The dachshund's rear end wiggled. There was a loud hissing sound. The dog quickly pulled its nose back, turned, and went scampering back across the street to its tiny doghouse.

"You'd better call your mother, Ned, and tell her where you are. She may be worried."

"You're right. I should have thought of that. Thanks." He walked over to the phone on the small table in the hallway. He lifted the receiver and dialed his home number.

His mother answered. George was crying in the background.

"Hi. Mom? I'll be home as soon as I can. I'll leave from Kathy's. . . . OK. Bye."

As soon as he had hung up, a series of three short siren blasts sounded. The three short blasts were repeated ten or twelve times.

"Guess we made it through another test, kid! That's our all-clear signal. Normal life can now resume in the nuclear town of Wilkenton. And I have to go home for dinner!"

2

After another quick kiss, Ned opened the door and walked out into the street and air.

The stillness—the silence—hung there outside.

Even though the all-clear signals had been given, no one except him seemed to be in any hurry to rush back out on the streets.

The sad-eyed dachshund watched him as he went quickly down the sidewalk.

Ned had enough time to walk home at a casual pace, but, instead, he hurried. He could barely keep from running. For some reason, he wanted to be home, inside his house with his mother and George, as quickly as possible. Though there seemed to be no danger—just another siren alert—he had to make sure they were safe.

Ned didn't want to admit it to Kathy, but those sirens unnerved him too. Even though he knew in his mind that this had just been another one of those tests, his heart pounded, raced, urged his feet to hurry home, to prove he

17

was right. He couldn't help himself. Once before, when those sirens had gone off and he had been away from home, he had imagined that his mom and little brother were dead, lying in there in the house. He had raced home then, too.

Now he cut across town from east to west. He could feel the cool air and winds sweep over the flat eastern Washington desert. The setting sun's rays bounced off the desert dust, setting off a scene of orange and red sky colors.

Less than twenty minutes later, Ned arrived home. He rushed up the front steps and hurriedly twisted the doorknob to open.

"Home! I'm home, Mom, in record time!"

His mom, still young, even though she *was* over forty, smiled. "In whose record time? Kathy's?"

Ned slumped down on a kitchen chair. "If it was Kathy's record time, Mom, I still wouldn't be home. I'd be at Kathy's. Maybe I should go back?"

She laughed. "No—no. I think you had better stay here. One record time a day is enough. I'm not sure how much Kathy might improve your timing."

"Is everything OK here? I mean, with the sirens and everything? Is George OK?" He looked out the kitchen entrance toward the hall and living room, but George was nowhere in sight.

"George could use your help right now. He started crying and ran to hide under his bed the minute those sirens went off. You know, just like he always has. I've been up to his room three or four times trying to get him to come out from under his bed, but he won't. And I'm just too old to get under there with him to bring him out. I need a nice older son for that."

"Poor George. Guess he's still under his bed then. Those sirens freak Kathy out too. She just stands there shaking and shivering all over when they go off."

His mom moved a pot from the sink to the stove. "Well, they're not the most pleasant sound in the world! And I could do without them and the thoughts they immediately bring to mind." She turned on the heat under the pot.

"Yeah. I know what you mean, Mom." Ned got up from the chair. "I'll go and see if I can help George."

"Tell him dinner is almost ready."

Ned slapped the doorframe with his hand as he left the kitchen, turned, and went up the stairs, two at a time.

He knocked on George's bedroom door.

There was no answer.

He knocked a little louder.

Silence.

But then as Ned leaned his ear closer to the door, he could hear low sobbing from inside.

Twisting the handle, Ned opened the door to George's room and walked in.

"George? It's me—Ned. How're you doin'? You OK, George?"

The sobbing stopped—and then started again.

Ned got down on his stomach on the floor. Peering under the bed, he could see a striped shirt huddled against the back wall. Every so often the shirt shook.

"Ah, come on, George. Come on out now. The sirens

have stopped. It's OK. Nothing's happened. Come on."

George sobbed a little more loudly.

"Hey! I know those sirens are enough to scare anyone—even me. I don't feel so good when I hear them either. Even Kathy doesn't like them. So, it's OK to feel that way. But they've stopped now. They probably won't go off like that again for a long time. So come on out of there."

George lifted his red, tear-streaked face and looked at Ned through the darkness. His two-year-old body looked much smaller covered by the shadows under the bed. But George didn't move.

Ned was too big to squeeze under any bed. Instead, he reached one of his long arms under the bed and grabbed George's small foot. Very easily and slowly, he began to pull George toward him, feet first.

When Ned had finally pulled George all the way out from under the bed, he and George lay side-by-side on the carpet. Ned placed his arm under the shoulders of his two-year-old brother and pulled him close.

"You're OK now—except your face is a mess. Let me wipe it for you." Ned reached into his pocket and took out a handkerchief. Gently, he patted away the tears around George's eyes, nose, and mouth.

"There! At least you look a little less like a red-faced monkey now—and more like any ordinary monkey!"

"I'm no monkey! I'm a boy! You're a porcupine!"

Ned looked shocked. "Me? I'm no porcupine! You're an elephant!"

"I'm no elephant! I'm a *boy!*"

"You are? You don't look like a boy," said Ned.

"I'm a *boy!* And you're a pig—horse—goose!" George rolled over, got up, and jumped on top of Ned's chest.

Ned made all the animal sounds. "Well, this pig-horse-goose is telling you that dinner is ready and that you had better get moving downstairs so we can eat. Or I just may eat *you!*" And Ned started tickling George until George fell off his chest and scrambled out the door.

3

Fifteen minutes later the three members of the Turner family sat at the table eating beef stew.

"Did you hear from Dad today?" Ned raised his eyes from his fork to look at his mother.

"Yes. He called this afternoon, just before the sirens went off. He's been very busy back there in D.C. since that Senator called and asked him to Washington for some special talks on nuclear plant issues. Guess he has lots to do." She took her napkin and absent-mindedly wiped the area around her plate. "Lots to do."

"But did he say anything about when he'd be coming home?"

She looked up at Ned and smiled. She knew how much he missed his dad. "He said he'd try—try very hard—to get home in a few days. Maybe fly to Spokane on Thursday and catch a ride back to Wilkenton from there."

"Hey! Great! I sure miss him. I never really knew how much I could miss Dad until he went away. Can't see why he had to give up his lawyer job to be a Representative! I mean, since he got elected last November he's been away most of the time. He's either in Olympia or somewhere else!"

George suddenly looked up from his food. Beef stew ran out of one corner of his mouth. Some had managed to land in his hair. "Daddy? Where Daddy? I want him."

His mother turned to George. "Soon, George. Daddy will be home soon."

"When home?"

"In a few days, George. Just a few days," she answered. "He'll be glad to see you—both of you." Turning back to Ned, his mother said, "You know we could have gone to Olympia with him and lived there. That's what your dad suggested we do. Remember? We asked you if you wanted to do that."

"I remember. But who knew it was going to be like this, with him gone so much and everything? Who wants to live in Olympia, anyhow? Who needs that?"

His mother pushed her chair away from the table and stood up. "Well, you made your decision—or, rather, we all made a decision to stay here. Now, as much as we miss your father, we'll have to live with that decision for a few years, I guess."

"I wanted to stay here in Wilkenton. I like it here. I like the quiet and openness. I can walk for miles without seeing another person—just by myself where I can think. The people are nice. All my friends and everything are right here." Ned stood up.

"I know how you feel, Ned. Those are some of the same

reasons your father and I don't want to leave here, too. You know, as far as living somewhere, he would rather be here in Wilkenton with us than where he is. But his job is there. Going on this trip to Washington, D.C., might be important for your father. State Representatives don't get invited to D.C. too often—not by important Senators." She and Ned collected some dishes and brought them to the kitchen sink.

"Hey! Me want down!" George wriggled and squirmed in his booster chair. He was stuck.

"OK, George. Just a minute. I'll be right there." Ned put the dishes down and turned to go back to the table. He lifted George up and out of his chair. "Yuch! Your hands and face are a mess! We'd better get you washed up."

"Lollipop! I want lollipop!"

"After you're washed up. Then we'll see about your lollipop. Let's go. Don't touch anything. You'll make it a mess, too."

Ned pushed George gently from behind down the hallway to the bathroom.

With a lot of spitting and sputtering from George, Ned managed to wash George's hands and face. George managed to soak Ned's shirt.

"Now, lollipop!" said George as he raced back to the kitchen.

Ned followed him.

After he had given George his lollipop, Ned's mother, who was at the sink washing dishes, turned and threw a dish towel at him. "Here. You can wipe."

"Thanks a lot. I needed this." Ned took the towel and picked up a glass from the dish rack.

"Oh, I forgot to tell you. Your father was asked to go to Washington to discuss heading up some citizens' committee for nuclear power—something like that. I guess they selected him because he's been so pro-nuclear power. Some Senators in D.C. want these pro-nuclear citizen committees to be formed all over the country to help promote nuclear energy. So they chose your father to form and head a local group here. I don't know what he's supposed to do on this committee, but he seemed pretty happy to be chosen and to be in with the Senators. I'm sure that the people at the Niconda Nuclear Plant and those from the Columbia Electric Company, who supported your father so much in his election, are happy about this, too."

"Well, that's good for Dad, I guess—and for Wilkenton and Washington, too. But, frankly, I'd rather have my dad home with me and let them keep their committees."

"It goes with the job, Ned. If he's going to do a good job—and that's the way your dad does things—then he just has to be away. I miss him a lot, too. But he still gets home a few times a month, you know. It's not completely bad."

"But he has another year or so to go with this thing! And what if he decides to run again? I mean—I could be in my mid-twenties or thirties before I get to have a dad again. Probably, by that time, I won't be at home for him to have a son! Maybe I'll never see him—just read about him and some of his speeches in the newspaper or see him on TV."

His mother turned from the sink to smile at him. "I think you're getting a little carried away about this whole thing."

Ned went on as if she hadn't spoken. "Some guy will walk up to me on the street one day and say, 'Great dad you have there. You must be very proud of him. Does a great job for us, son, supervising those nuke plants.' What would I say to the guy? 'If you say so, sir. He's really close to those atoms! All I know about my dad is what I read in the papers or see on TV.' Great!"

"Easy, Ned. Take it easy on your dad. Remember—we all sat around the kitchen table and discussed the whole matter. Your dad felt strongly about the Niconda plant and how beneficial it has been for this town. He believes in the future of nuclear power as our major energy resource. We felt that he would be a good representative for this area, one who would stand up to the emotional scare-tactics of those antinuclear demonstrators and voices that have been getting more and more attention. Remember that? We agreed it would be rough for us as a family, but that it was a sacrifice we all could live with for a few years."

"Yeah. But that was then—before he actually won this thing and went off to the state capital. I mean, how was I supposed to know he'd actually win this thing and be a State Representative? He'd never run for any type of elective office before. It seemed like just some kind of game, you know—a contest you enter but don't ever expect to win, a thousand-to-one shot. I didn't know—"

"Ned, who did know when we first talked about it? We worked with your dad on his campaign—folding letters, making posters, and all the other things. You should have known that when your dad says he is going to do something, then he does his very best to do it. He's always been that way—all out to finish what he starts. And when the plant people from Niconda finally threw their support behind him as their chosen candidate—well, their support tells all in this town."

"Yeah, but—"

CRASH!

George had managed to pull down a whole shelf of pots and pans.

4

Jack Abinson, the physics teacher at Wilkenton High, unrolled a long chart from the top of a stand.

"Since we have the Niconda plant here in Wilkenton, and since it affects our lives so greatly in more ways than we may realize, it seems a good idea to spend some class time studying about nuclear power. At least we can give you some basic information so you have some idea about what's happening inside those thick concrete walls."

Ned leaned over to Kathy. "Now, we're going to get some high-powered stuff. If you don't understand this, don't ask me! I won't understand it either!"

Kathy leaned over and patted him on the head.

Mr. Abinson looked from the chart to the students. He chewed on his lip for a second. "This may take some effort for you all to understand, but I think it's worth a try. OK. Here goes!" He lifted his pointer and moved to the side of the chart. "At the center of any nuclear reactor is the core. This core usually has in it Plutonium-239, made from Uranium-238. This is the fuel or fissionable material. 'Fission' refers to the splitting of atoms. Now, Niconda has a fission reactor. Got that?"

Mr. Abinson looked up from his notes.

Ned saw twenty-three heads bob up and down, his own included, saying that they understood. Ned knew he didn't, and he knew that most of the others didn't understand either.

"OK. Look. Fission is just a splitting—like you split open an apple. Only in this case, you're splitting open these invisible atoms. When they are split, they set off heat and radiation. Right?"

Again, Ned and the others bobbed their heads up and down.

For the next thirty minutes, Mr. Abinson tried his best to explain about splitting atoms, and how the energy that splitting sets off is used to heat the water in the plant pools, which in turn work the steam turbines to generate electricity. "That electricity goes to homes, factories, and businesses in a good part of the state of Washington."

Fred Peterson, a boy who spent most of his class time either picking his teeth or scratching his head, waved his hand in the air. "I don't get it. Do you mean just cracking those tiny atom-things—that you can't even see with one of those high-powered microscopes—that cracking those atom-things lights up everything in half the state?"

"Something like that. Splitting the atoms begins the process, Fred. The turbines eventually send electricity to heat our homes—and even this school." Mr. Abinson smiled.

Ned felt that he almost understood, but he was getting

one whale of a headache almost understanding this.

"Now, we should look at the benefits and some of the problems with splitting these invisible atoms. For example, why do these invisible atoms have to be surrounded in all that concrete? Why the sirens and bullhorn warnings? What's happening around here? Anyone care to answer that?"

SueAnn James' hand went up. "It's because of all that radiation. If you get near that radiation—right up close—the heat alone would burn you to a crisp. You know, fried human, very well done!"

"You're right, SueAnn. It's the radiation that's our main concern. It—or the heat from it—really could fry a human to a 'crisp,' but only if a person came in direct contact with a heavy dose of it. If that radiation escapes into the air or ground or water, it won't fry you, but it can possibly kill you or make you very ill. If the radiation escapes, it could contaminate everything for maybe one-quarter to one-half of this state. That means water, land, plants, animals, and people. Nothing would escape being contaminated from radiation. Plus everything would remain contaminated for twenty or thirty years, or even longer. In effect, the contaminated part of the state would probably be a wasteland with little or no life of any kind."

"Heck!" said Ned. "Some people think this part of Washington is a wasteland already—except for a few people living out here. But with the plant here it's doing OK."

Kathy raised her hand. "But, if there's a chance that all that radiation could get out into the air or water, why do we have nuclear plants? Why do they take a chance?"

30

"Money! Money! Money!," chanted Fred from behind her. "Money is the power, honey. This little desert, nothing town of once a few hundred has more than tripled in size since that plant came to town. People here have all kinds of good-paying jobs, and the taxes that plant pays build your schools, roads, and football stadium. Don't you know that, baby?"

"What Fred says is right, Kathy. This town has benefited a good deal from the Niconda plant. But—" Mr. Abinson paused to pace once across the front of the room—"I share some of your concerns and questions, too. Are the risks involved in having that plant here and operating worth the benefits the townspeople receive? The more I read about the safety problems in nuclear plants, about accidents in other plants in the nation, about what we don't know with regard to controlling atomic power, the more concerned and worried I become."

Mr. Abinson appeared to become lost in his own thoughts for a moment.

The class seemed suspended, waiting to be led forward.

"Well, back to basic physics—and away from morality." Mr. Abinson picked up his pointer again and walked back to the chart. "As the chart tells you here, radiation is measured in millirems. Got that? Mill-i-rems. OK? Well, that's how they measure the amount of radiation. The average person in the United States receives about 100 millirems of radiation each year. This radiation comes from the sun's rays, your fancy radium dial watches, the I'm-in-a-rush microwave ovens, and from the color idiot boxes."

"Hey! Tell us," broke in Jake Anders, the class clown. "Do

you get to be more of an idiot getting radiation from a color idiot box than from one of the old black-and-whites? Or do you just break out in technicolor spots?"

The usual four or five giggles came from the group in the back of the room, Jake's followers.

Mr. Abinson gave them a little smile of recognition. At least the remark showed he still had the interest of the students in the back. "Well, Jake, I'll let you consult with a child psychologist on that one—or a skin doctor."

The bell rang.

Everyone started shuffling books and feet, and getting up from their seats. Mr. Abinson was still talking.

"Wait a minute. Hold on. I have one thing more to say before you go."

Students stood around, annoyed that they couldn't go charging out the door. You'd think they had some big race to run, instead of just going on to their next class.

Ned stopped moving. He reached out to take Kathy's hand. They both waited to hear what Mr. Abinson had to say.

"Let me just tell you that tomorrow we'll have a guest speaker in here to talk to you about nuclear plants. He's Carl Hinders, a supervisor out at the Niconda plant. He'll explain some of the special safety features out there, the daily routine, and answer any questions you might have. So have some questions. OK? Think about what that nuclear power plant means to you. Think about how safe it really is and what would happen if there was some type of major accident. That's all. You can go now."

Ned and Kathy joined the shuffling, shoving students.

They even managed to squeeze through the door still holding hands.

Ned wondered how many of the students had heard Abinson's last words. Once the bell rings, everyone tunes out the teacher.

5

"Do you know this guy Hinders that Abinson said was coming to class tomorrow?" Ned asked Kathy as he steered her down the hall toward the library.

"I've met him once or twice. He's a friend of my dad's at work. He seems like a nice guy. He does some public relations things for the plant—like coming here to speak. The time I heard him speak to a women's group my mom was in he sounded pretty convincing." Kathy picked up their walking pace so they'd make it to the library before the period bell sounded.

When they arrived at the library door, a student aide checked them in and had them sign their names and the time on an attendance roster.

Once in the library, everything went down to a whisper, the way people would talk if they went to a funeral or a church.

"Let's sit down here near the 800s and 900s. I've got to do

a report on Henry VIII." Ned dropped his books down on the table. The sound echoed through the stillness of the library. Two dozen heads popped up to see what the noise was and who had dared make it. Ned froze. The librarian aide just frowned and went back to sorting catalog cards.

Kathy gently placed her books on the table and sat down in a chair next to Ned. "Watch me. I'll teach you how to behave," she whispered.

Ned sat still in the chair for a few minutes, gathering some historical energy inside to begin his report. Then he got up from his seat and started searching through the books on the shelves. Kathy sat and read.

A little while later, Ned returned with six large books. "Let me tell you! That Henry got mentioned everywhere! He led some kind of life—or wife, depending on which wife he had at the time. And I haven't even checked the biography section yet!" Ned put the books down—more quietly this time—and sat down in a chair.

Looking up from her book, Kathy gave him a brief smile. "Maybe reading about all those wives will help your husbandry instincts."

"Help them! At least Henry can show me how to get rid of a wife—one way or another!"

"Divorce got old King Henry into a lot of trouble. Remember? When he couldn't chop off their heads, he got stuck for alimony." Kathy turned a page in her book.

"And, if we should marry sometime, would you prefer to have your head chopped off or be sent to a nunnery?"

"I refuse to choose! Now, let's get back to work, sir."

They each read quietly for a while.

Then, Ned's arm encircled Kathy from behind, and his fingers began to crawl up her arm.

"Ned! Stop it! You're tickling me. Cut it out!"

"Who, me? Tickle you? Never!"

"Ned! Cut it out—and get back to reading."

His fingers played with the back of her neck.

Kathy placed her book face-down flat on the table. "What do you think you're doing?"

"Well, I thought about measuring your millirems. Would you like me to do that?"

"To do what?"

"Measure your millirems. Don't you want to know how much of my radiation you can take?"

She turned to look at him. "I know how much of your radiation I can take, thank you."

"Obviously, it's not enough. I haven't seen you glow in the dark lately."

"Try me." Kathy poked him in the ribs.

Jake Anders came from behind them and leaned right in between them. "Follow me," he whispered, "for the chance of a lifetime. Just come right this way, and you may win a small fortune."

Kathy and Ned looked at each other and then at Jake. They both shook their heads.

"Now, now," Jake said, patting Ned on the shoulder, "you wouldn't want to miss this chance. Believe me. This may make you worship sirens. Follow me."

Kathy and Ned looked at each other again, shrugged, and got up. They followed Jake in and out of the stacks of books

36

until they came to a hidden corner of the library. Three other boys were there.

Jake took out a long, yellow, legal-sized pad. "What you see here is a chance to win some money. Maybe a lot of money—$10, $20, or $30 even. It just depends on how many suckers we get."

"Hey, Jake! If you mean we're to be some of those 'suckers,' that's not the way to sell a contest or future customer. Let me tell you, buddy," said Ned.

"What do you mean, son? Didn't P.T. Barnum say 'There's a sucker born every minute'? That means there's a lot of them suckers all around the place."

"Great! Thanks a lot." Kathy put on one of her sarcastic smiles. Ned enjoyed watching her go into her act. When she really got angry, she could give anyone a good tongue-lashing, even Jake the mouth. "So, now, you have two more 'suckers' here? Well, I don't like being called a 'sucker,' Jake Anders. I don't know what you're up to or why you dragged us over here to whisper in the corner of the library, but I don't think I'll stay to find out."

"Wait—wait a minute—just hold on. Not you, girl. You two aren't suckers. I mean—well, you can tell suckers from—from people like you. Sure, you can. People like you know what's happening. We communicate—the three of us—we know each other. I didn't mean you."

Ned laughed. "You certainly know how to grease your mouth, Anders. You twist things around that you might choke on, and they just come sliding right out."

"You might call it smooth-talk, Ned," Kathy said, glancing

sideways at him, "but I just call it a lot of hot air."

"Well, we'll see if we end up being played for suckers or not. Tell us, Jake, old buddy, what's the deal here?" Ned played with Kathy's fingers as they waited for Jake's explanation.

"OK. It's simple—real simple."

"You mean simple enough for even us suckers to understand?" Kathy said.

"I'll ignore that and go on with my sales pitch." Jake turned from Kathy and concentrated his talk on Ned. "What we have devised here is a little game of chance. All you do is pick some dates—dates when you think that crazy siren might go off again for one of its tests. OK? And you also have to pick a time of the day—like January 5, 8:15 A.M. See?"

Ned nodded his head. "Yeah. You pick a date and a time that the sirens might go off. So?"

"Well, each person that does that throws in fifty cents per day and time. And the one who comes closest when that thing sounds off wins the pot. You gotta figure that for fifty cents a throw a lot of kids will want in on this. The pot will really add up."

"How much do you have now, Jake?" Kathy asked. "And do we get some kind of receipt for our contribution?"

"Receipt? Well, I guess that could be arranged, my lady. Sure, if you don't trust me, my notebook and my solid memory, I'll give you a receipt. OK? And there's about $7 in the pot now."

"And you're going to hold the money and be good for this?"

38

Jake looked at Kathy and laughed. "Hey! What is this girl, the IRS or something? Do you think I'm going to run to Mexico with $7 or so? Do you want me to walk into the principal and say, 'Here's our pot, Mr. Principal, will you hold our gambling money in your lap until we find out who wins it? Will you keep it safe for us, sir, because Kathy here doesn't trust old slick Jake?' Is that what you want, girl?" Jake laughed again. "Oh! That man would just love it, wouldn't he? He'd absolutely love it!"

"Why, all Kathy's trying to do, Jake, is to protect our investment. You can't blame her for that. She's a shrewd woman—that's why I go with her. She handles all our business transactions." Ned ran his fingers up Kathy's back as she squirmed away.

"OK. Look—about the only thing I can do is to give my solemn promise as a student in poor standing here at Wilkenton High that I will not run to Mexico, Canada, or China with your money. Besides, some of the guys who put in money already would take me apart limb from limb if I tried any funny business. You know? And I like myself all together too much. So, do you want to play and put some money in or not?"

"Well, Jake, it is sort of a weird thing to bet on. What if those sirens went off and it was for *real*—not just a test. Crazy sort of way to win a bet." Ned looked from Jake to Kathy.

"Don't worry—don't worry. All the money will be kept in a lead pouch, guaranteed to be radiation-proof. No *hot* money in this deal. Guaranteed. Besides, those things have never gone off for real before. They just let them screech out every month or two to keep them and the people in town in shape."

"OK." Ned reached into his back pocket for his wallet. "Just because you're crazy enough to do something like this, I'll be crazy enough to put some money into it. Here's two dollars." Ned couldn't believe he really was getting suckered into a scheme like this. But there was something about Jake—and Jake's crazy schemes and ideas—that always seemed to appeal to Ned. Jake was different. He was a unique character and his own kind of person.

"Fine. Now, you have four dates and times to pick."

Ned thought for a moment. "Give me October 29 at 9:45 A.M.—and November 4 at 7:30 P.M.—and December 25 at midnight—and, Kath, you pick the last one. I'm worn out from dealing with this shark."

"You do know how to throw away two dollars. I hope you don't come along and tell me now you can't afford to take me out Saturday because you are short of cash. Remember, I was there! OK, try November 26 at 7:00 A.M.—just in case I want to sleep late that day and cut a morning of school."

"Fine, fine! You're down for those dates and times, my friends. You may be lucky enough to win yourselves a small fortune."

"But what happens if the sirens—for some reason—don't go off? Maybe they get broken or maybe there's no need for them to go off—no more testing or something. What happens then? Do you keep the little fortune, Jake?"

Jake waved her off. "Don't worry your pretty head about

that, girl. Those sirens—they always have gone off since the feds got more uptight. They'll go off again in some test in one or two months' time. You can bet on it. You can bet your life on it, girl."

Kathy stared at Jake with a humorless expression. "Thanks. But I'd rather not."

6

The bell sounded, ending the school day.

Ned and Kathy got their jackets and books from their lockers. Hand-in-hand, they walked out of school and down Main Street, the only main street in Wilkenton, toward the center of town.

As they neared the shopping and business district, Ned could feel the added tension in the air.

Off in the distance, they could hear the noise of a large group of people. Then they could see signs waving in the air.

The scene became clearer as Ned and Kathy skirted the border of the supermarket parking lot.

Five or six pickup trucks and some vans had parked in the lot. Eighty or a hundred people were milling around at one end of the lot, while another dozen or so helped unload signs nailed to pieces of wood. Some took out pamphlets and flyers from one of the vans. One or two had small movie cameras and were taking pictures. A Spokane news camera-man and reporter stood off to the side.

"I forgot the paper said that the anti-nukes were coming to entertain us again. They come here from their polluted city holes to bring us their junk mail, litter, signs, and crazy ideas. Now that really makes sense!" Ned stopped on the sidewalk twenty yards or so away from the main group of demonstrators.

Kathy remained beside Ned. "Let's see," she said. "This must be about the fifth or sixth time they've been out this year. I really think it's sort of like a picnic for most of them. You know—like 'Let's go out to the desert and picket the old nuclear plant. Come get some sun, some laughs, some singing and group chants—and think what we'll be doing to save all those poor misguided people.' I bet they even de-duct this trip from their income taxes!"

Ned shook his head. "It's strange, isn't it? They've been out here so many times, and they've never changed any-thing. Plus, with the engineering and safety features that have gone into that plant, nothing's gonna happen. They should know that there's no real danger from the plant, that everything is under control there, closely watched. Yet, they keep coming back."

He paused to watch them some more. "You know, there never seems to be more than about a hundred of them. Re-member when all the TV cameras and reporters came with them the first few times? Now, the news people don't bother to come out much either."

"The scary thing is that sometimes I think this could get out of hand. Remember, Ned, wasn't it just two months ago on a march here that some people from town went out after the marchers? Just followed behind them and started yelling things at them? Later, that night, they found some guy—in his twenties—beaten up in an alleyway behind the tavern. He had stayed behind or something after the other marchers had left."

"Yeah. I remember. Too bad that people get so angry and do something like that. But that guy knew he wasn't going to be too popular around here if he stayed—at least, he should have known. You might say what you want about other issues in Wilkenton—the president, taxes, welfare, whatever—but you don't come out and say anything against our nuclear plant. Not if you're smart—and want to stay in one piece."

The marchers began moving across the parking lot toward one of the pickup trucks.

Ned's head popped up straighter. His eyes followed one of the marchers. "Look at that girl, will you? The one over there. Now, she's not bad-looking! What's she doing in this thing?"

"I don't look at girls carrying picket signs, Mr. Turner!"

"Well, I mean, usually you don't expect a good-looking girl like that to be out there carrying crazy signs in the hot desert—and everything like that. You don't think she'd be—"

"*You* don't think! I dare you to go and tell her what *you* think! Go on! I'd like to see what happens." Kathy pushed him toward the group of demonstrators.

Ned backed off.

Just then one of the leaders climbed on a pickup and, using a megaphone, called the group together.

44

"OK. Now, remember we're here for a peaceful demonstration. Have your signs up, sing, chant, tell anyone you can about the dangers of nuclear power and these power plants, but don't bug anyone. Try not to get people uptight—because then they don't listen. Also, we don't want any bloody heads again. Don't give the cops any excuses for getting on us. No damaging property. If we get arrested and thrown in jail for trespassing on the plant grounds, that's the way it goes. But that's all."

The man giving the speech loosened his tie. The tie hung down from an open-collared shirt. He was maybe in his late twenties or early thirties. Ned couldn't tell, but he did admire the man's coolness, his poise. He seemed to know exactly what he was doing, what he wanted to do, and what could happen.

Ned also watched the girl move up toward the front of the crowd until she was directly in front of the man speaking. She looked up at the man. Her red hair hung down to her shoulders, and occasionally she'd brush away some strands of hair that blew over her cheeks. She wore a red print shirt tucked into tight-fitting jeans. As she listened to the guy's speech, she let her sign hang down to the ground, upside-down. Ned had to almost stand on his head to read it. It said, "Hell, No! We Won't Glow!"

Leaning over his shoulder, Kathy whispered, "You could always just walk right up to her—close—and tell her you're far-sighted and couldn't read her sign. Go ahead. Don't mind me."

"So," continued the speaker, "we are all ready now to get going. We need one van and one pickup to drive alongside us. Leave the rest of the cars and trucks here. Get on your walking shoes, folks—for those of you who are new to this. It's a five-mile hike over hot, dusty, rock-hard desert land to the Niconda plant. The only water around is the river near the plant—and I wouldn't want to drink *that* water no matter how thirsty I was. Fill your canteens."

While some people went over to the water barrels on the truck to fill their canteens, the man stepped down from the pickup truck. He put his hand around the redhead's shoulders and said something to her. She laughed. Then the two of them moved aside to let people load a few barrels of water onto the truck.

Ned found himself watching the two closely, wondering about who they were, and if she was his girl or not.

"Line up four across and let's march right out there. Here we go!" The man picked up a sign and led the group from the parking lot out onto the main street of town. They carried their signs high. Some read, "Stop Nuclear Power Before It Stops You!," "Too Much Heat for Future Generations," "Don't Fry Me Now—Don't Cancer Me Later!," "Will Light Now Help You See the Future?," "Save the World for My Children."

Ned saw that the red-haired girl held her sign right up there with the rest. She was in the middle of the group now, and marched right by Ned and Kathy.

This was the first time that Ned had been close to one of these demonstrations before. The other times there had been demonstrations, Ned had felt that he had wanted to stay as far away from them as he could. He was afraid, in some way, that they might contaminate him, threaten him somehow.

"You know, Kath, it's funny but if I wasn't so sure that they were wrong about Niconda, I could almost get caught up in all this—from just what we've seen today. It's sort of— of hypnotic. Do you feel that way?" Ned finally turned his head from the marchers to look at Kathy.

Kathy looked at him and shook her head.

"Well, couldn't you, Kath? Wouldn't you like to just follow along to see what happens—to see what it's like?"

"If you mean would I like to follow that redhead who won't glow to walk five miles and watch her wiggle her rear around in those jeans out there? No, thanks! Redheads built like that just don't interest me. Male ones might, but this one—no."

"No? Really, Kath. Would you go along just out of curiosity?"

"I'm just not that curious—and I certainly don't want to be out there if things start to boil up and over and bodies start to fly."

"Do you think that might actually happen? You think people from here would go out there and start something with those marchers—even though some of them are women, boys, girls?"

"I think so," she said. "I think that if people get angry and worried enough, if outsiders come in here to stir things up, then, things happen."

Ned stood there silently, looking out toward the last of the marchers disappearing into the desert. "I guess I can see your point. I mean, I know these people here pretty well, but I guess, with outsiders, they might do something you wouldn't think they would do."

Kathy took his hand and tugged him lightly into walking toward her house. "Let me tell you, my bright—brown-haired—naive friend, it's bad enough for the outsiders who dare to come here and march. They leave together afterward in a group. I wouldn't want to see an 'insider,' a person living in this town, ever get involved with those marchers. It would be the end for him. I heard my dad and some of his friends from the plant talking one night at our house. They as much as said that if you live in Wilkenton, you had better be a Niconda person and love that plant—or leave town fast. They didn't want any traitors in this town. And I think they had in mind someone they thought was a traitor."

"Who?"

"I don't know. They never mentioned a name."

Ned looked at her face closely to see if she was hiding the name from him. "You really don't know who it was? Well, I hate to think of someone trying to undermine the plant in this town! They'd probably kill the guy!"

Kathy nodded slowly. "Come on. We'd better get me home fast. It's late. Besides, your redhead is out of sight—but probably not out of mind. So, are you going to walk this dull-haired brunette home?"

Ned leaned over and nipped Kathy on the ear.

"Ouch! What do you think you're doing? Animal!"

"I think I'll walk the brunette home—the dull one. I like the taste of brunette ears better."

48

"That's 'dull-haired,' mister. And the ears stay on the head. Come on. I'll glow for you."

They looked up to find a woman in her mid-twenties holding out her hand with a pamphlet in it. She was one of the demonstrators not marching, but informing instead. "Here you go. Why don't you just read about nuclear power and nuclear plants? They affect you and your families—and any children you may have—in more ways than you think. It's your future and theirs. Did you know that in that Niconda Nuclear Plant they have a fission reactor, and may soon have a breeder reactor—one of the most dangerous types of reactors?"

Ned looked at her and smiled. "Why, I thought that the Planned Parenthood Association took care of all those breeders."

The woman didn't laugh. Obviously, she just didn't have a sense of humor about nuclear breeder reactors.

7

When they arrived at Kathy's house, Kathy's mother ran to the door to meet them.

Her mother, a plump woman with short brown hair, wearing a loose print dress, put her finger over her mouth to warn Ned and Kathy to be quiet.

"Hey! Mom? Why are you home from work at the bank? Something wrong? You sick?" Kathy dropped her books down on the small table in the entrance hall.

Her mother didn't answer, but, instead, waved the quiet-finger at them. She motioned to them to follow her into the kitchen.

Ned looked from her mother to Kathy.

Kathy had a puzzled, worried expression.

"What's the matter? Is it Dad?"

Her mother nodded.

"What's wrong with him? What's the matter? Tell me, Mom."

Ned pulled one of the kitchen chairs out away from the

50

table and steered Kathy toward it, so she could sit down.

Her mother came over to Kathy. She put her arm around her daughter and hugged her tightly. She sighed deeply, but didn't say anything.

Ned shifted back and forth from one foot to the other. He nervously waited to hear what had happened to Kathy's dad. At the same time, he wondered if he should stay here. No one spoke to him. He just watched mother and daughter. No one suggested he leave. They seemed to have forgotten he was there. He felt like a Peeping Tom in on some personal family matter.

"Your father, Kathy, came home because he wasn't feeling well. He says he has a very bad upset stomach. He doesn't look well to me at all. Maybe it's more than just an upset stomach. Maybe it's something he got from being in that nuclear plant. Who knows what it could be, Kathy?"

"Well, did anyone at the plant look Dad over? Don't they know if it's radiation or not?"

Her mother gave one of her dramatic sighs again. "Who knows? Who knows? Your dad says they examined him. He said they told him it was just some dizziness and stomach cramps—maybe the flu. They *think* he should be fine in a few days. But who knows?"

"What do you mean 'who knows?' Did you call his doctor? How does Dad feel now?"

"I called—I called the doctor. The doctor said he doesn't know anything about radiation. The doctor said that they have doctors at the plant, and that those doctors know what they're doing about radiation. That's what he told me when I called. Then I called out to the plant and spoke to one of the doctors there. They said it wasn't radiation—just the flu or something—that's what they said. But I don't know whether to believe them or not. I don't know." Her mother stood up, clutching her hands together.

Ned walked as quietly as he could around the kitchen. He looked at the calendar, some pots and pans, and out the window. He tried to pretend he wasn't hearing all this—unless they showed that they wanted him to be part of this scene.

"Can't he or you tell anything about what's the matter?" Kathy asked.

Her mother didn't seem to hear her question. "They called me at work—at the bank—to tell me that he was being sent home. They seemed concerned. When I heard that I had a call like that from the plant, I thought he was dead. I really thought he was dead. With that radiation there—and possible accidents, even small ones—and no one can see it, you know—no one—I thought he was dead—"

"Mom, it's OK. They said he'd be all right. I know it frightened you—frightened you a lot, but it's OK. They have doctors there. I bet he just has a bad stomach and a little dizziness. That's all—right?"

"I've always been afraid—always afraid. That radiation scares me. Whenever I mentioned it to your father—told him I was afraid—he'd laugh and say it was no more dangerous than a lot of other jobs he's had, and that other people have. That's what he'd say—"

Ned had backed himself into a corner of the kitchen. He stood by helplessly, awkwardly, as he watched the scene between mother and daughter. If Kathy and he had been alone, he might talk with her, help in some way. But with her mother there he felt he had no right to butt in.

"Kathy? Is my Kathy home?" The voice of her father sounded strained and tired.

Kathy turned away from her mother, who had stopped her rambling speech when she heard Kathy's father's voice.

"Where is he, Mom?"

Her mother lifted her right hand and gestured toward the living room. Then, her hand fell heavily to her side. She sat down in one of the kitchen chairs.

"I'm coming, Dad—be right there."

Kathy ran into the living room. Ned walked behind her.

Her dad was there lying on the couch on the far side of the living room. He was covered with two blankets, his head propped up by pillows. He made no effort to get up when he saw them.

Kathy ran to his side and knelt down on the carpet. She took his hand and held it tenderly in her own. He reached from under the covers with his other hand and stroked her hair.

"You look as worried as your mother did. I'm just a little tired."

"But you look so pale and weak, Dad. What happened? What kind of accident?"

"There was no accident, Kathy—nothing to worry about. I just have the flu—or something. I feel weak, dizzy, nauseous." He gave a short laugh. "With a little rest and attention around here, I'll be back on my feet in a day or two, and working again. Don't worry yourself. It's just the flu, and it's hit me really hard." He patted her hand reassuringly.

Kathy looked into his eyes. They still had their twinkle, that "I'm-not-afraid-of-anything" sparkle. If something happened that wasn't too good, he'd find some way to laugh about it, even if he had been the butt of the joke.

"You—you spoke with the doctors? They examined you?" she asked.

"Yes. They did. They went over my old body from head to toe, geiger counter and all. They said I didn't have any radiation problems. Besides, the radiation exposure badge they make us wear would have given me away if I had gotten a dose somewhere. It looks like they'll be right again. I'd bet on it."

"Again? What—what do you mean 'again'?"

"Well, Kathy, I've had one or two little accidents in the time I've been working up there. Nothing's fool-proof, no matter how much people plan and try or how careful everyone is. Accidents just happen. I've been in a few, and usually had no really bad effects from them—maybe some dizziness or stomach problems, a headache or two. That's all. But I didn't really even get my badge exposed this time."

Ned listened. He watched and listened. There were accidents up there! Could there be such a thing as a "small nuclear accident"? When does it become "not so small"?

"There's nothing really to worry about up there, though. They have enough controls and checks and safety measures to prevent anything really big from happening. But small things just happen once in a while."

Kathy laid her head on her father's chest.

"Uh—well—uh. I hope you—you feel better, Mr. Jenkins. I have to—to get going now." Ned moved off toward the front door.

Kathy turned her face to look at Ned as he went. Mr. Jenkins raised a hand and waved. His pale face gave a weak smile.

Ned paused for a moment at the front door. When Kathy had problems like this, he loved her all the more. He wanted to comfort and protect her from whatever was hurting her. Even now, he thought she would know he was waiting, that she would come running up behind him and give him a kiss.

But she never came.

Ned opened the front door and closed it behind him.

8

She hadn't arrived at school when classes began the next day. As a matter of fact, the first class Ned had a chance to see Kathy in was their fourth period physics class. And she was even late to that.

Ned could still see a grim look on her face. She looked tired, as if she hadn't slept the whole night.

"How are you doing?" Ned whispered to her as she sat down at her desk next to him.

"OK, I guess. Just tired. Couldn't sleep last night. Just had horrible dreams—nightmares—awful."

Ned placed his hand on hers. "How's your dad doing?"

"He seems better. Got out of bed this morning. He even said he felt like going to work today, but we wouldn't let him. He said he wasn't dizzy or anything, but the plant called again to make sure he stayed home for at least another day to rest. They're nice about that. I mean about letting you rest if you're sick." Kathy opened her notebook and searched for a pen.

"Here. I have an extra pen you can use. You must really be tired, and distracted. I think this is the first time you've not had notebook, books, homework, and pen all out and ready for a class."

She gave him a little smile.

Before Ned could say anything else, Mr. Abinson stood up in front of the room. He had just completed his attendance check. "May I have your attention, please. We have, as I told you, a special guest today—Mr. Carl Hinders, who works in the personnel and public relations section of the Niconda Nuclear Plant. He's here to talk to you about nuclear energy—what it can do and its problems. He'll try to answer any questions you may have also. So, with your cooperation, I'll turn the rest of this class period over to Mr. Hinders."

Ned watched a small man, about five and a half feet tall, with black-rimmed glasses and thin gray hair, step forward from the corner of the room. The man was dressed in a neat, expensive, gray-striped suit. He walked solidly, with confidence. He turned at the center front of the room and smiled at the class. Despite his size, when he began to speak his voice was surprisingly strong, dynamic, and clear.

"I'm Mr. Hinders. I work in the personnel department at the Niconda Nuclear Plant. As you can see, one of my jobs is to do some public relations work for the plant. I have spoken to a number of groups in the community—and enjoy doing so. This, however, is the first time I have addressed a high school class.

"Mr. Abinson has informed me that you have some basic information about how a nuclear plant works. I would like to describe that for you in more detail. Then, perhaps, answer some questions—but, please, I prefer to complete my presentation before you ask those questions. Therefore, I trust you can refrain from interrupting.

"At the Niconda plant, you first must note . . ."

Ned wasn't too interested in hearing more details about how the reactor worked, and how fuel was used. But that's what Mr. Hinders talked about for the first twenty minutes of the period. Ned tried to listen, but found himself drifting. He looked at Kathy several times, but she had her head on her books most of the time and seemed asleep. He didn't want to disturb her.

Fred Peterson leaned over and whispered to Ned. "If this guy lectures to all his audiences like this, I bet none of them ever ask him back again. PR is not his big thing! He's cold—very cold."

Ned nodded without turning around.

". . . safety measures are one of our prime concerns. We are well aware that we are working with a highly dangerous material. We must protect ourselves, the plant, and the people in the area. . . ."

Ned waited for him to add the phrase "not necessarily in that order," but Mr. Hinders didn't add it.

"I'm glad to report that there is nothing to worry about. Everything is made safe, checked and rechecked. Nothing and no one gets by without being in top shape. Around the reactor itself where the fission occurs, we have 59-foot-high walls of steel and that steel is $11^5/_8$ inches thick, enclosing and sealing the reactor." He waved and jabbed his finger at the class. "We have a dome around the reactor, too. It stands 240 feet high and 190 feet across. It has a wall of concrete six feet thick over a wall of carbonized steel. In addition to all this, we have several water cooling systems to cool down the reactor, and giant pumps will rush the water in at the punch of a button from one of the men in the control room."

When he had finished his speech, he looked around the room at the various students. He smiled, pleased with himself, as if he didn't really expect any questions. But, he asked anyway, "So, do you have any questions?"

The students looked at one another, but no one raised a hand. After that speech, Ned and the others felt too tired to bother to ask questions.

So, Mr. Abinson asked, "What happens if these cooling systems don't work? What then?"

Hinders chuckled at that thought. "That, of course, could hardly ever happen. We simply have too many backup systems for such a thing."

"Just out of curiosity and information for the students," added Mr. Abinson, "would you tell us what *would* happen?"

"Well, in theory, I could tell you what would happen if every backup system failed to operate. Remember, this is just in *theory*. If the water level dropped too low, the core— the fuel—of the reactor would become exposed. Well, if the nuclear fuel became too hot, it could—would—melt, like wax or chocolate. In theory, it could melt down right through the bottom of the reactor container. This would produce what is called the 'China Syndrome.' Remember, they used to say you could dig your way through the earth to

China. Well, with the nuclear fuel some imaginative engineers have put forth the idea that the nuclear fuel could melt its way through the earth to China. So, the 'China Syndrome.' There wouldn't be any explosion, as many people might think, just a melting. Any explosion would have to be a gas or steam explosion, which is highly unlikely. In *theory*, such an explosion might rupture the containment building."

Mr. Hinders paused.

Ned was listening now, as were many of the others. He tried to understand, to picture in his mind in some way what Hinders was telling them—in theory.

Mr. Abinson cut in again. "If there should be—in theory—such an explosion and the containment structure should be shattered, what would happen?"

Something in his teacher's voice, his tone, made Ned turn around and look closely at Mr. Abinson. He could see that Mr. Abinson seemed tense—literally on his toes—ready to pounce on someone or something.

"Radioactive gases and other radioactive particles might escape into the air." Mr. Hinders' face became hard and fixed.

"And then, Mr. Hinders, how would we know if these gases escaped, and were dangerous?"

Mr. Hinders cleared his throat twice. "Most likely, the average person would not know, Mr. Abinson, because radioactive gases cannot be smelled, seen, or tasted. They are, for all intents, invisible. But, of course, we monitor everything. We would alert the community through the siren system established and the mobile horns. That's why we constantly test them and have them in readiness—even though we are sure they will never be necessary."

"And these radioactive gases that escape, where would they, or could they, go—in theory, of course?"

Ned saw that Mr. Abinson had focused his complete attention on Hinders, as if Hinders were some animal he wanted to trap. It seemed as if his teacher had forgotten completely about the class he had in the room. It was some sort of contest between just the two of them. Ned kept looking from one man to the other, trying to determine exactly what was happening.

"The gases would be in the atmosphere around the plant."

"Yes. And how far could these gases be carried? I've been doing some research, you see, so let me save you the trouble of answering that question. According to what I've read, these gases could be carried thirty to forty miles in any direction. When they eventually settled to the ground, they would contaminate everyone and everything they touched—and they would be invisible."

Hinders didn't reply. He just stared.

Kathy had roused and lifted her head up. She sat up straight in her chair, alertly listening to the verbal combat.

"In a melt-down—a China Syndrome," said Mr. Abinson, "the radioactivity would seep through the soil and into the air, contaminating everyone and everything. I—"

"Excuse me, Mr. Abinson, but my time is short. All that you have mentioned and described is theoretically possible, but, as I have indicated, highly unlikely—impossible."

"Yes, I understand. But if the unthinkable—the catastrophe—did happen, it would be so great that it would be difficult to imagine. A whole community—possibly half a state even—could be wiped out, rendered a complete wasteland for decades—"

Hinders turned away from Mr. Abinson. He began putting some papers into his grained-leather briefcase. He zipped the case closed.

"Have you heard about the near disaster at the Fermi nuclear plant, near Detroit, Mr. Hinders? Do you know that over four million people would have been trapped in that area—exposed to a nuclear accident? Only sheer luck prevented a disaster. I read somewhere that an MIT scientist who had studied the near disaster at Fermi stated something that we all know—or should know. He said that people and equipment have always been, and will always be, subject to failures, mistakes, and breakdowns. Do you agree with that, Mr. Hinders?"

Mr. Hinders straightened his tie, but did not respond.

Ned noticed two different fires in each of their eyes. Mr. Abinson's eyes had lit up shining; an energy came from them. Mr. Hinders' eyes smoldered with sparks flaring every so often.

"And he also quotes an insurance executive who said that there is a serious question as to whether the amount of damage to persons and property—from a nuclear catastrophe—would be worth the possible benefit accruing from atomic development. Tell us, Mr. Hinders, is it worth the risk?"

Hinders clasped his hands behind his back. "In my opinion, and in the opinion of many others, it is more than worth the risk. The risk is small—but your friends there are entitled to their opinions, though they seem overly excitable and hysterical."

Kathy raised her hand. She looked soberly at Mr. Hinders.

When Hinders saw her hand go up, he immediately turned to recognize her. It would be a relief from Mr. Abinson's attack.

"Mr. Hinders, are there accidents—small accidents—at the Niconda plant?"

Hinders looked at her, confused about Kathy's question.

"I mean accidents, like radioactive water splashing on workers from pipes, or gas leaks, or something else. Do they happen that often, to people in the plant? Accidents that we never hear about?"

Hinders cleared his throat. "I'm not exactly certain about what you mean, young lady. If you mean are there some small incidents at Niconda where a worker gets cut, falls, may touch a drop or two of something radioactive, that does happen—but very, very seldom. Those sort of things will happen in any type of factory or plant. Coal miners suffer from black lung disease—and some die from it. Asbestos workers have had health problems. We have had very, very few in comparison."

Kathy tried hard to follow Hinders' answer. Ned could see the effort in her face. He knew why she had to know—why she needed an answer.

"What happens, Mr. Hinders, to someone who has a few accidents with radioactive materials in the plant? Can they die?"

"If anyone has that many accidents with radioactive materials, we'd probably fire him or her long before they died. We have doctors there—specialists—who watch over the workers' health. Besides, if anyone registers a large dose of radiation in their bodies, they would not, by federal regula-

63

tions, be allowed to work near nuclear materials again."

Kathy wasn't about to give up. "Could someone die from touching those radioactive materials?"

"Die? Well, I guess if they stayed too long or had an extremely high dosage and exposure to them, then they might die. But that has never happened. Radiation affects people in different ways. Some studies indicate that people in contact with radiation would have an increased risk of cancer later in their lives. How great that risk is, no one's certain. They've shown that cancer can be caused by any number of things, including some of the manufactured food we eat. Accidental contact with radiation is one possible cause only."

"But it *could* happen, Mr. Hinders?" Kathy leaned forward over her desk. "Someone could die from too many accidents—and accidents do happen at Niconda?"

9

The end-of-the-period bell rang.

To Ned, it sounded like the ringside bell to end a prize-fight—except that he wasn't too certain what the prize was.

The other students got up from their seats and left the room.

Ned watched Kathy. She didn't move from her seat. She just kept staring straight ahead toward Hinders, but he could tell her mind was far away and not on Hinders at all.

He leaned over toward her and placed his hand softly on her shoulder. "Come on, Kath. It's time to go. It's over here, Kath."

She didn't seem to hear him.

Standing up, he gathered his books under his arm. He felt tired, drained. "Come on, Kath."

He reached down and grasped her under the arm and helped her to her feet. Finally, she reached over for her books and picked them up.

Once the other students had left and only Ned and Kathy

remained, the room remained strangely silent—except for Ned's whispered words.

Mr. Abinson stayed in the back of the room, leaning against some bookshelves, his head bent, eyes focused on the tiled floor. He seemed deep in thought.

Ned saw that Carl Hinders hadn't left yet. Ned would have thought he would have gone out that door as quickly as possible. Instead, Hinders kept rearranging papers inside his briefcase.

Ned and Kathy moved quietly between the two men. They crossed over to the door.

Ned stopped at the door and turned to look at each man—his teacher, and the guest speaker. In his mind, he tried to come to grips with what had happened in class. It was more than just a guest speaker presentation that could be easily forgotten. Mr. Abinson seemed to have made some sort of decision, almost a plan, of what would happen. He was the first teacher in Wilkenton—the first person in Wilkenton—that had dared, as far as Ned knew, to speak out against Niconda and its nuclear power. Ned wasn't too sure how much of what Mr. Abinson had said was true. After all, Hinders was the expert. He worked there; he was trained to speak on nuclear power and Niconda. Would Hinders work in a place that could be that dangerous, risk his life and the lives of so many people living near the plant? Would the government allow such a plant to be built and to operate if it could lead to such a disaster? Certainly not. Too many people in important places—the president, senators, congressmen, scientists—would stop it.

Ned shook his head and turned back to leave. He heard

Mr. Abinson say, "I should thank you for coming, Mr. Hinders. The class did enjoy your presentation. It was informative." Mr. Abinson said most of this with his head still bent to the floor. Toward the end of the words, he lifted his eyes and looked at Carl Hinders.

"Did they enjoy it, Mr. Abinson? I thought that, perhaps, they enjoyed your performance even more. But, I can't say that I did." He closed his briefcase.

"I'm sorry about that. I may have gotten a little carried away with my point of view. I wanted the class to understand that there are two sides to the issue of nuclear power. I have some serious concerns about its uses and safety."

"I became aware of that. I feel I was used, Mr. Abinson, by you so you could get on your antinuclear platform. I was your scapegoat."

Mr. Abinson sighed.

"I didn't appreciate it at all, Mr. Abinson." Hinders picked up his briefcase and coat and walked toward the door. "Not at all." He pushed between Ned and the doorway, and walked down the hall.

10

At ten o'clock that evening, Jack Turner, State Representative—and Ned's father—came home.

The doorbell rang. The door chimes even overcame the sound of the TV.

Ned reached the door first and opened it.

His father stood there, raincoat slung over his arm, suitcase at his feet, and a briefcase in the other hand. His sandy hair was windblown, his gold-rimmed glasses had slipped down, balancing lightly on the tip of his nose.

"Well? How have you been doing, son?" His dad wrapped his arm around Ned's shoulders and pulled his son toward him.

It felt good. Ned liked it when his dad held him like that. It felt like everything was OK—back to normal again. They were a family.

George ducked between Ned's legs and bumped headfirst into his dad's knee. "Ouch! Your knee hurt me! Why did it do that? Bad knee!"

68

Jack Turner let go of Ned and bent down to scoop up his youngest son into his arms. "I'm sure my knee didn't mean it, George."

George locked his arms around his dad's neck.

"Easy, George, or you're going to choke your old dad before he even gets into the house."

Ned saw his mom waiting inside the house, happily watching the welcome home scene, and letting everyone else get their greetings in first.

"Where's your mother, boys? Is she lost somewhere?"

Jack Turner picked up his suitcase and walked through the front doorway, with George still hanging from his neck.

"Oh! There you are! Why, I thought you'd run off or been kidnapped. Such a quiet woman I married!"

Ned's mom smiled.

For Mom, Ned's dad put down his coat and suitcase and briefcase and wrapped both his arms around her. They kissed and then, after another hug, he let her go.

"It's good to have you home and back in my arms, Mr. Representative. Your family's been waiting—and so has your coffee."

Dad sat down on the couch. Ned sat next to him. George scrambled up to sit on his dad's knee.

"So, what have you two been doing? What's been going on here in Wild West Wilkenton? When I was back in D.C., the people there still thought the Indians were on the attack!"

"You're joking, right?" Ned said.

"Not by much," replied his dad. "People back there still don't know much—at least some of them—about the West.

The only associations they have are cowboys and Indians."

"New Spideyman. New doll. You want to see?" George got off the couch—headfirst—and landed on the carpet. Then he ran away to get his new doll. Dad never got a chance to answer if he wanted to see the doll or not.

Ned watched George run off. "Nothing much has been happening here. You know—I mean—what's to happen out here in the desert of Wilkenton? We still have the usual people coming here from Oregon, Idaho, and sometimes California to walk through Main Street and out to Niconda. They get their kicks out of carrying their dumb signs and marching along. . . . Although, some of the protesters are getting better-looking—like this redhead I saw. Now, she wasn't bad!"

His dad grinned. "I see, a redhead. Well, maybe she'll be back and bring a blonde along, too. Those protests are going to keep on going for a long while. So, keep watching."

"We did have this discussion in class on nuclear power and its effect on all of us—in physics class. Even had this guy from Niconda come in and talk to us, but . . . well, Mr. Abinson, you know—my teacher—he sort of got really carried away."

"What do you mean?"

"Well, he started bringing up all these things about how dangerous nuclear plants are. I mean, he was really going after this guy—like attacking him."

"And? What do you think?" His dad turned a little to look more directly at him.

"I . . . I don't know. I can't believe all of what Mr. Abinson was saying. I never heard those things before. The other guy's the expert. He's the one who should know."

"There's a lot we *both* have to learn about nuclear power yet."

"It was strange, Dad. I didn't feel good about what happened in that class."

"Yeah, I can understand. Tell me, you still seeing Kathy?"

"Sure. Every day at school and after. We're still going together."

Mom came in with a coffee pot in one hand and a tray with cups and plates in the other. "Here you go. Be right back with some Pittsville cherry pie."

"Oh, bad pun, Barbara! After a long trip, I have to come home to listen to that? Better be careful. I may leave again."

From the kitchen, she said, "No idle threats, dear. I'm sure you *will* leave again. So, eat the cherry pie I'm bringing and enjoy it, pits and all."

In came the hot cherry pie. Dad ate it. So did Ned.

"So, tell us about this new job you have, Jack, on that nuclear citizens' committee." His mom sat down in the stuffed chair near the couch.

Jack Turner put down his coffee cup. "It's just political. There's a nuclear plant here. They're looking for people who are mainly pro-nuclear plants and energy. I'm the State Representative here, so the politicians thought it would be good to have me on this committee. I've been pro-nuclear and Niconda backed me solidly in my campaign—so that's the job I got doled out to me."

"What will this committee do, Dad? It *will* do something, won't it?" Ned asked.

"Good question, Ned. I'm not sure what all we will do when we get organized and working. In general, we're supposed to respond to citizens' concerns about the plants and about nuclear energy. We also help them understand what Columbia Electric says is going on at the plant. Then we could question Niconda or Columbia people about what they're doing. We must have some type of influence with the Senate, I guess. After all, Senators were the ones who asked us to form some type of local pro-nuclear committee. I'm not sure what else we'll be doing. They're supposed to let me know and send me more information. Maybe I'll jog over to see how they're doing at Niconda tomorrow—just to stick my nose in before I take off for Olympia again."

Ned patted his dad on the knee. "Sounds like an easy enough job, Dad. You can handle it."

"Thanks—for your confidence. Well, I guess if there's any problem at the plant, I'd be the one to go up there and ask some questions from a citizen's point of view. We could organize to bring strong pressures to have a plant shut down to make repairs or to make them safer if there were accidents. I don't expect to ever have to do something like that, though—not with all the safety systems they have in those plants."

Ned's mother wrinkled her forehead. "That could be a little dangerous, couldn't it, Jack? If there's something wrong in the plants, you mean you have to walk right in there and find out what it is?"

"Possibly. But I'm sure if it were serious, they wouldn't let us in. They'd inspect everything first and check it out. They wouldn't want to see any up-and-coming Representative contaminated."

"You sure about that, Dad?"

"What do you mean, 'You sure about that, Dad?' Some son I have! He wants to see his old dad light up with a radiation glow!"

"I didn't exactly say that."

Dad smiled. "Oh, I see. Well, anyhow, I just probably will investigate, along with whomever I can recruit as the other members for this committee from around the Wilkenton area."

"Have there been any problems, Jack? Have they closed down any plants because of radiation accidents?" Ned's mother had that concerned look on her face.

"Some problems, Barb. But don't worry. They've usually been caught in time and controlled. There haven't been any major catastrophes yet from a nuclear power plant in this country—none I've heard of. The rest of the people heading up similar committees throughout the nation seem to feel that nuclear power is developing well. A few plants may get a small leak, have a gauge break, or need a pump repaired— but no large amounts of radiation or gases seem to have escaped and done any damage. The NRC has only closed a few plants in the last ten years or so. Most plants, like the one here, close down on their own, anyhow, two or three times a year for cleaning, repairs, and inspections."

"Easy job, Dad. No sweat."

Dad nodded. "Yeah. It does sound easy enough. Not exactly challenging or demanding. Doubt I'm going to make 'Representative of the Year' in the 'Washington State Government Official Beauty Contest' with a job like this. Maybe it's too easy. After a year, I'll try to get out of this or at least get on some committee that does more. Hate for this to be my entire political career: Mr. Jack Turner, State Representative Nuke-Pusher."

"You'd better watch those catchy phrases, Dad. You almost sound like one of those sign-carrying marchers."

"Anything but that, son!" His dad laughed.

George came running back into the room. He tripped and something went flying out of his small hands.

"Spidey—Spideyman—he all twisted up. What a mess! Daddy, you fix him. You know how. You fix everything and make it right."

His dad took Spideyman and carefully began to inspect the damage done.

11

A holiday—especially a Friday holiday—meant another protest march. With a three-day weekend, marchers could come from even farther distances away. Ned had seen a sign once that mentioned Boulder, Colorado. How the person had gotten all this way for a march Ned didn't know.

Few demonstrators came from that far away now. The Niconda marches didn't seem to spark much interest anymore. Even most of the townspeople in Wilkenton ignored the small group turnouts. It wasn't worth getting all that excited about.

A Friday holiday without Kathy was boring. She had had to go off to visit some relatives in Spokane. If she had been here with him, they would have walked and picnicked in the desert—had a nice day. She always made him chocolate pudding. But there was no Kathy with him.

Ned stood inside the grocery store by the magazine rack, looking out at the gathering crowd of protesters in the warm afternoon.

Then he saw the girl again—the nice-looking, redheaded one. She walked by the outside of the store, swinging her hips. She stopped by the door, placed her sign against the window, and came into the store.

Ned followed her with his eyes as she went down the candy aisle to find a pack of gum and then over to the fruit aisle for an apple.

As she came back toward the check-out counters, the manager stopped her.

"We would appreciate it if you would leave the store and remove your sign from the front of this store—immediately." He glared down at her.

She smiled back. "Yes. I will—but *may* I buy these things first?"

"Quickly. Just pay for them and leave."

"Yes, sir! Right away, sir!" She went toward the speed-out checker. Then she stopped and called back to the manager. "These aren't contaminated, are they?"

The manager didn't answer. He stalked away stiff-backed.

As she waited at the counter, she turned in Ned's direction.

He quickly pretended he was reading a magazine.

Ned saw that she was looking right at him—and laughing. He flushed. It was only after she had turned away to pay the cashier that he noticed he had picked up a *Good Housekeeping* magazine to read.

Out of the store she went and picked up her sign. Then she paraded three times right in front of the store, the words on her sign "You'll Never Know Until It's Too Late" flashing full at the customers inside the store.

The infuriated manager was just about to go after the redhead when she turned and crossed through the parking lot to her friends and fellow marchers.

Ned couldn't help laughing and shaking his head in wonder at her brashness and spunk. He would never have done something like that.

The same young man Ned had seen before stood in the back of a pickup and spoke to the crowd. Ned couldn't hear what he said from inside the store, but he could see his gestures and the response on the faces of the marchers.

Ned moved to the door and walked outside. He leaned against the building, observing the organization for the protest march.

Suddenly, from the corner of his eye, he saw a familiar figure standing on the back edge of the crowd listening to the speaker. This figure had a sign like most of the others had. Ned turned to face the person far across from him.

It was—it was Mr. Abinson, the physics teacher! Mr. Abinson was standing there with a sign. He was actually going to march with them! Crazy! He's crazy, Ned thought to himself. A townsperson had never been with these marchers. Abinson wouldn't be able to live or work in Wilkenton once he marched on the Niconda plant.

Mr. Abinson didn't shout and cheer with the others. He didn't wave his sign in the air and rush to line up three abreast. Instead, he stood there quietly, firmly, resolute. He knew what he was doing. This had to be far more than a holiday fling for him.

At a hand signal from the man in the truck, the marchers moved in formation down Main Street, through town, and out the road toward the plant.

While Ned stood there watching, two men came out of

the store. The men stood five feet or so away from Ned and they also watched the group leave.

"Look at them. Bunch of troublemakers, that's all. We have to put up with them coming to our town to hold their little parades."

The second man laughed. "Guess you haven't heard, but rumor has it that they're going to get theirs today out there—real good they're going to get it."

The first man waved the second off. "Yeah, I've heard that before, but only one or two got beaten up good. And that didn't stop them."

The two men crossed over into the parking lot and climbed in a blue sedan.

Ned didn't think much about what he had overheard. Just a lot of hot air, probably.

He watched the end line of the protesters move down the road. Without Kathy, he didn't know what to do with himself.

He kicked a few stones the width and then the length of the parking lot. Finally, he started walking—walking across the desert parallel to the marchers, walking toward the Niconda plant. Why he was walking there, he didn't know. Call it curiosity, interest, anything—but it *was* the best show in town.

12

Ned lay down face up on the top of a small hill overlooking the Niconda plant.

He had crossed the arid land, arriving at this hilltop shortly after the protesters had arrived at the plant. For the past thirty minutes or so, he had stood, sat, and lay there watching the people below yell, chant, sing, and go around in endless circles in front of the plant's main gates. How long they planned to keep the circling going he didn't know.

The parklike entrance to the plant, with its tall spindly trees and rolled grass top, made a sharp, ironic contrast to the dry land surrounding the plant. Ned knew the plant got its water from an underground river flow. Some of the water was used in the plant, some was diverted to create a fertile place for an artificial park of trees and grass. If the farmers had had the money to bring the water to the arid land, the land would grow almost anything. But they didn't have the money. The federal government did—and they had brought the water to the nuclear reactor instead.

The direct rays of the bright sun made Ned shut his eyes. This last time he had shut them he had fallen asleep.

Ned awoke and opened his eyes when he felt the sun's rays suddenly blocked from his face. He saw a silhouette—the figure of a young woman standing over him in front of the sun.

Ned squinted, looking up.

The voice of the silhouette said, "What's your name? What are you doing up here?"

"Ned—Ned Turner."

"And what are you doing here spying on us?"

"I wasn't 'spying.' I was just watching—curious—that's all. There's no law about not sitting in the desert watching a protest march, is there?" Ned didn't know why he was answering questions like this. He belonged here; this girl didn't.

Then the silhouette moved to the right. The sun's rays struck him full in the face and Ned turned his eyes and face down.

She—the redhead he had seen in the store—flopped down beside him.

"Well, hi, Ned. My name is Jane Sollis. I go to Specter Creek High, just outside of Spokane. You know where that is?"

Ned nodded. "Like a suburb."

He felt confused. Ned didn't know whether to sit here next to this girl, this protester, or get up and walk away back across the desert. So he didn't move.

"It's nice over there. Lived there for eight years now. Quiet and peaceful—sometimes too quiet and peaceful," she said, and flashed him a toothy smile.

Ned sat up, clasping his hands around his knees. "I—ah—I heard there's a lot of art people there. You know, like writers and painters and people like that."

"Yeah, there are a lot of interesting people living there. Some people from there organized this march. They have sort of an antinuclear group at Specter Creek—and some of us from high school are members. So we go along on these things."

Ned nodded his head in understanding, but said nothing. He felt clumsy, awkward, klutzy in this girl's presence.

"Well," she said in a somewhat exasperated voice, "aren't you going to ask me why I'm with this group, what I'm doing here, don't I have better things to do with my time, a young girl like me?" She tossed some pebbles down the side of the hill. "That's what most people ask me first."

Ned shrugged his shoulders.

"Well, let me tell you, Ned Turner, I'm here because I *want* to be here, because I *believe* in this cause. I don't want my world messed up—destroyed, contaminated, producing deformed babies—because some scientists and businessmen make money off the people playing around with nuclear fuel that could destroy all of us. We're not that desperate for nuclear power."

"You know, you sound like that guy in the pickup truck who leads you. Almost word-for-word, you sound like him."

"I can't help that. He's just saying what we believe—and know to be true."

Ned stretched out his legs. "But how do you know?"

"I read, Ned Turner. I read books, magazines, newspapers that discuss the whole nuclear power thing. They talk about the need for energy, but also about the dangers of nuclear fuel, its radioactive wastes, the chances of human error setting off an accident that could wipe out half this state, and the possibility of terrorists seizing one of the plants. I read."

"But aren't those just things written by people who are against nuclear power in the first place? Are you sure they're the right facts? I haven't read much antinuclear power stuff."

"You! What do you read? *The Wilkenton Press?* Who do you think *owns The Wilkenton Press?* Who owns most of the people in this town? Niconda—that's who! You think they'd allow this town's paper to print antinuclear stories? Do you think the editor, who wants to keep his job, would do that? No way, friend. They're all in this together. They live high as long as that potential bomb here with its reactor is running." She got to her feet.

"OK. The plant means a lot to this town, but nothing serious has happened. We've never had any problem—and the people out here seem to know what they're doing, have alert drills, and all that."

"If a major accident happens, there might not be any second chances—no time to say 'we never had any problems before.' Wait a minute. You said your name is 'Turner,' didn't you? Your father isn't Jack Turner, the new State Representative from around here, is he?"

Ned swallowed hard, "Yes, he is. So what?"

"And didn't I read somewhere that he'd been appointed to some Nuke Super Committee?"

"That's right."

"Well, then, he should be out here with us. He must know the facts, know the dangers with these plants. Why isn't he here marching on this place with us? He could be a big help. He's supposed to be so concerned about the *people*'s welfare—"

"Why should he be out here marching? He's *for* nuclear power. He thinks it will help the energy crisis, help the people."

She reached down and brushed off some desert dirt from her jeans. "You mean, he's just like all the others here? In Niconda's pocket—or pocketbook?"

"Wait a minute! He's in no one's pocket. He believes in nuclear power. He's entitled to his opinion, too. Not everyone has to follow your propaganda."

"I hope he wakes up and sees what that plant could do— before we all get killed. Anyhow, it's been a real pleasure talking with you."

"Do you mean 'lecturing' me?"

She laughed. "Yeah, I guess so. Well, I have to rejoin the group down there. My coffee break time is up. If you're still on this hill when we have a lunch break, I'll maybe come back."

"For another lecture?"

"Maybe not," she smiled, and started down the hill. At the bottom of the hill, she turned and waved to him. Ned waved back. He saw her pick up a sign again and join the circle of marchers.

He was thirsty. They had water down by the marchers, but he didn't want to go down there to ask for some. He didn't want to get involved with them.

Mr. Abinson still walked round and round in the circle, gripping his sign and holding it high. He never seemed to stop, relax, or talk to anyone else there.

Ned picked up a blade of dried, brown grass and let it

dangle from his lips. He looked over at the giant blocks jutting up from the desert crust. They seemed to be in some sort of pattern, he thought—like you could worship there. Stonehenge came to his mind. Just like the pagan temple at Stonehenge with its great stones. Someone had to bring those great stones to Stonehenge just like someone had to bring these giant concrete blocks and cylinders to the desert of Wilkenton.

People went in and out of those cylinders day and night, but few ever heard about what went on inside there. Few could understand. You just had to accept it on faith—that they knew what they were doing.

13

Swirling desert dust from a car and two pickup trucks caught Ned's attention.

One pickup came to an abrupt, squealing halt.

Men jumped out from all three vehicles—big men, some with clubs.

Ned's stomach tightened when he saw them. He knew this meant trouble—the trouble he had heard threatened when he was at the grocery store.

The protesters watched the men. Their chanting and singing became louder, a higher pitch. Hands gripped the signs more tightly. No one stopped their circling.

These men—a few of whom Ned had seen hanging around town—moved closer to the protesters.

Ned thought he should leave—get out of there before the trouble began—but he couldn't. He had to stay and see for himself what would happen, especially to the girl and to Mr. Abinson. For some reason, he liked her, despite her hard line of talk, her brashness.

One of the men from town called out to the marchers. "Creeps! What are you doing here? Get out of town! Get out of our town and our plant. Now!"

"Look at that fat one over there. Maybe we can get him to *eat* his sign. Just shove it down his throat." This brought a chorus of crude laughter.

"Do you think they're all stoned, or just looking for trouble?"

"That one there. The redheaded young one in the tight jeans. Now, she ain't bad. Don't know what she's doing with these other jerks, but I'll carry *her* sign—or carry *her*, too!"

"Yeah! She's nice. We could all help her out of here."

The protesters ignored the baiting from the men. They kept a tight circle and continued walking, singing songs about sunshine and green valleys.

Ned's hands started to sweat from the tension in his own body. Jane held her head up and walked straight, but he knew their yelling about her must be getting to her. Ned knew it was only a matter of minutes before someone would blow this whole thing apart.

He clenched his fists, hitting them against his thighs in frustration. Then he turned to go—to cut back across the desert and the hill—just to get away from this place. He couldn't do anything about it anyhow. Jane and Mr. Abinson had made their choice.

As he began to walk down the back side of the hill, he caught a glimpse of someone coming out of the plant toward the gate to talk to one of the guards.

Ned stopped. He looked more closely. Yes, it was Hinders—Carl Hinders there.

Hinders watched the protesters. Then he seemed to lock in on one particular protester. He spoke to one of the guards again and pointed to one of the men from town.

The guard walked over to a man wearing a plaid shirt. The guard pointed to someone in the circle of protesters. Then the guard returned to his place at the main gate.

The man in the plaid shirt went over to some other men from town, and spoke to them and pointed.

The men started in with their name-calling again—only this time with a specific purpose.

"There's one among you who's different—a different kind of creep. He's a *towny* creep! Comes from right here—from *our* town—and marches with *you!* That's not healthy!"

"Yeah. That commie teaches our kids. Can't have something like that around here. Have to stamp it out!"

Mr. Abinson flashed a quick look at the men, but he didn't stop walking. Ned could imagine the sweat pouring down Mr. Abinson's face. But he seemed to raise his sign even higher above the others.

Ned felt a sense of pride for his teacher. Mr. Abinson was doing something he believed in—and wasn't about to let any bullies frighten him or chase him away. But Ned was afraid for him, too. Mr. Abinson wouldn't stand a chance against even one of those big guys. He wouldn't stand a chance.

"Guys like that shouldn't be allowed *near* kids. They're weird. Can't trust what they'll do next."

Ned thought, Why shouldn't a man like Mr. Abinson be teaching kids? Didn't Mr. Abinson have a right to express his own opinion in a peaceful way? Didn't he have a right to say what was on his mind, teacher or not? And didn't kids in school—have a right to hear different opinions and make up their own minds about what they believed and wanted to support? Wasn't that part of what learning's all about?

"Well, we got to protect ourselves and our kids. We'll *do* something *now!*"

Somewhere from the back of the group of men a rock flew through the air. It landed a foot away from Mr. Abinson. He kept walking at the same steady pace.

Ned froze there, watching the scene below, a few hundred feet away.

Ned thought that Mr. Abinson had seemed fierce, almost violent, in his verbal attack on Carl Hinders in class the other day. Now he looked strangely small—fragile.

The second rock hit Mr. Abinson in the forehead. It cut him and some drops of blood trickled down the side of his face. Still, he didn't stop walking. He didn't say anything. He didn't even look at the men to find out who had thrown the rock, and he didn't try to stop the blood from running down his face.

Ned reached in his pocket to feel for his own handkerchief. He was ready to run down there to offer to help Mr. Abinson stop the bleeding.

"Good hit!" said a rough voice from the roadside, "but you can do better than that."

The voice sounded like a coach psyching his football team up to make them more vicious when they had a chance to attack the opposition.

The rocks started to fly at the protesters.

The signs went down to cover people's heads and faces from the flying rocks.

The circle broke.

The townies moved in. They tripped the men and women protesters, grabbed their signs and ripped them up.

Three of the bigger men had isolated Mr. Abinson. After ripping his sign from his hands, they knocked Mr. Abinson to the ground and started punching and kicking him. He was helpless. He couldn't protect himself from all the blows.

Ned moved a few steps toward the edge of the hill. Then he broke into a run. In a moment, he was right in the middle of all the fighting.

Ned was at the side of Mr. Abinson's attackers. He brought a fist down on the back of one of the men who was bent over, punching at his teacher.

The man lurched forward off-balance and fell to the ground. A minute later he was up again.

Another one of the attackers spun Ned around, placed the heel of his palm under Ned's chin, and pushed him backwards. Ned went flying, and ended up sprawled on the ground.

He heard a short, high-pitched scream, followed by "No! Leave me alone! Don't touch me." He looked through the flaying arms and legs, punches and curses, to see Jane. She had fallen to the ground, too. A squat, fat man stood over her.

Ned scrambled to his feet and ran toward her.

As the man bent down to grab Jane by her blouse, Ned came up behind him. He shoved the man forward, and the man went sailing, face-first into the hard ground. He lay there stunned.

Ned reached down and took hold of Jane's arm. She seemed dazed. He pulled her up and, quickly, pushed her off toward the desert and the hill.

Jane stumbled forward. Ned kept her from falling. She was crying. The tears ran over the dust and scratches on her face.

No one followed them. In the confusion of people beating up other people, and the yells and the dust, Ned didn't know if anyone had seen him push the man down and take Jane away.

They reached the top of the hill. Then he helped Jane sit down.

Ned looked back at the scene below. The fighting had stopped. The townies moved back to watch the protesters lying still or weeping on the ground. Signs, sticks, pieces of clothing lay scattered around. The big men had satisfied smiles on their faces.

Ned saw that Mr. Abinson lay off to the side, curled up in a ball, rocking back and forth on his side in obvious pain.

Ned wanted to go down to Mr. Abinson again, but he didn't know if he should leave Jane.

"I'm OK—nothing but a few scratches and bruises. Thanks—thanks a lot, Ned." Jane looked up at him, shaking her head in an effort to clear her mind.

"My—uh—my teacher—he's down there. They beat him up. If you're all right here, I'd like to go back down—and—and try to help him—somehow."

Jane tried to smile, but her lower lip had puffed out. "Go on. Help him. I'm fine."

As he started down the hill, Ned caught sight of the main gate shutting and the form of Mr. Carl Hinders disappearing into the great concrete towers.

From miles away, he could hear the sirens—two different

kinds of sirens, one the police, the other the ambulance. Whoever had called them, finally, from inside the plant had certainly wanted the townies to get their licks in first.

When they heard the sirens, the townies laughed and patted one another on the back. They climbed back into the pickups and the car and sped away.

What was the sense of it all? Ned wondered to himself. The protesters come out here knowing they might get beat up or thrown in jail—just to carry some signs around in a circle in front of a locked gate. They didn't even have a chance to speak to anyone at the plant, anyone who would listen to their concerns. Who sent those townies, the big guys with the clubs, out here? Why beat up these people like this? They weren't doing any harm to the plant. Why mess up Mr. Abinson that way? For revenge? It just didn't make sense.

Ned's head pounded. He felt dizzy. Must be from all this time out in the desert sun.

He took out his handkerchief and wiped the sweat from his forehead. He looked back at Jane. She sat there, knees tucked under her chin, staring bitterly at the scene below.

She stood up. "Let's go down and help them."

Ned walked back to her and placed a hand on her shoulder. "The medics are there now. They know what they're doing. We'd only be in the way. Let's just go. Let's get out of here."

They both went down the other side of the hill and headed out across the desert.

14

Several hours later, Ned arrived home.

He felt choked with dust—dry and depressed. He was so dry that he didn't stop to speak to anyone in the house. He just nodded to his dad and continued walking up to his room, and then to the shower.

When he and Jane had arrived back in town, he had taken her to the local hospital for some first aid for her bruises and scratches.

The hospital waiting room in the outpatient area seemed jammed with patients, people from the demonstration who had been beaten and bruised. A few had been beaten badly enough to be carried in on stretchers. Most just had some cuts, bruises, ripped clothes, and black eyes.

Ned had waited with Jane for almost an hour there—silently—both thinking their own thoughts, but not saying a word to one another.

The nurse finally came, examined Jane, and then brought some medicines and bandages to treat her.

"Jane, I—uh—I have to get going. You OK now? Will somebody be here to take you home?"

She had nodded wearily. "I'll get a ride with someone in here. Don't worry—and thanks."

Ned had patted her on the shoulder, and left.

The bullets of hot water hitting his face, chest, and back felt indescribably good. They seemed to let his body—and mind—breathe again. They wiped away, for a few moments, the images of the desert, the beatings, the sobbing of a red-haired girl.

He turned off the water and reached for a towel.

Some afternoon! he thought. How did I ever get into all this? All I was doing was taking a simple walk downtown, just to kill some time. It was lonely without Kathy. He rubbed himself hard with the towel, making his body redden until it stung.

And Jane. How did I ever get involved with her—dragging her out of that mob? He smiled, remembering the scene of Jane marching in front of the store flashing her sign to the people inside. That was great!

He took some fresh clothes from his closet. A flash-picture came to his mind of Mr. Abinson. He saw the men knock his teacher to the ground, the men beating him, and, from the distant hill, Mr. Abinson lying curled in a ball on the ground rocking back and forth in pain. Ned shook his head to clear his mind of that memory.

He opened the bathroom door, and then went down the stairs to find his dad.

15

His dad sat in an overstuffed chair in the study, hidden behind a newspaper wall. It was a *New York Times* wall— the sports section.

"Dad? Can I speak with you about something—something that happened and maybe you should know about?" Ned stood to one side of the newspaper wall.

The tone of Ned's voice made his dad lower the newspaper pages to his lap. He looked at Ned. "Sure, son, pull up a chair and let me hear what you have to say."

Ned picked up a wooden straight-back chair and placed it down in front of his dad's chair. He sat down on it, crossing and uncrossing his legs.

"Well, Dad, you know they had another one of those nuclear protest marches out at Niconda today?"

His dad nodded. "Yes, I heard there was going to be another one. I also heard some rumors about trouble for the marchers. I didn't like hearing that."

"Yeah. Well, I sort of ended up out there at the plant

when the protesters were there. I didn't go as part of the march or anything—I just—sort of wandered out there out of curiosity and boredom. Then I, accidentally, met this red-haired girl. Very nice! She was one of the marchers."

"From the way you say 'nice,' I take it you are not just referring to her personality." His dad smiled.

Ned blushed.

"OK, son, so go on."

Ned shifted restlessly in his chair. He could talk with his dad pretty well—his dad seemed to listen. But sometimes Ned didn't know if he was talking with dad the lawyer or dad the Representative, or dad his father.

"So, when I got there, the protesters were already going around in circles in front of the main gate of the plant. They weren't doing anything to the plant—not even really blocking anyone from getting in and out of the plant. Well, then, that trouble that you heard about—it happened. These trucks with big men in them—some with clubs—came. Most of the men I'd never seen around here before. They were really big guys!"

His dad's face grew more intent and serious.

"When I saw them yelling like that and getting closer and closer to the protesters, I knew there was going to be trouble. Mr. Abinson, my physics teacher—he was one of the protesters. I knew there was going to be really big trouble for him—in this town. Anyhow, this guy Hinders, who spoke at our class that day—remember?—well, he came down to the gate and pointed out Mr. Abinson to the guard and to the men from town."

Ned paused to catch his breath.

"Then, it all broke loose—rocks flying, signs ripped up, people knocked down and beaten. Three of those guys jumped Mr. Abinson, punching and kicking him. I went down there to try to help him, but got knocked away, and then I heard Jane scream, and went to help her. This big, fat guy was on top of her. I knocked him down and we ran for the hill. No one followed us."

His dad leaned forward and placed his hand on Ned's arm. "It's OK, son. Go on—finish it."

"There's nothing much more to tell. I looked back and saw all these people, who weren't harming anyone or anything, lying on the ground beaten, weeping. And poor Mr. Abinson, he really looked in bad shape, rolling on the ground in pain. Why did they do that to him? Finally, the police and some ambulances came—but those guys got clean away long before."

Ned stopped, exhausted at having to relive the whole thing again and tell someone else about it.

His dad didn't say anything. He just sat there in silence, looking at the wall in back of Ned.

"Why did they do that, Dad? Why did those guys come out there and start beating on people like that—men and women, even girls? Why?" He looked at his dad's eyes for an answer.

Slowly, his dad said, "I don't know, son. You say these men were from town?"

"Well, some of them were. I've seen some of them hanging around the local bars or on the streets."

"I guess, Ned, some people just get carried away. They get so worried that people with different opinions might

threaten them—like close down Niconda Nuclear Plant—
that they'll do most anything to get rid of that threat. In this
case—and I've heard of this a few times before—it was beating up these protesters. I just haven't heard about anything
this bad before now—just an individual fight or two, that's
all.

"You can't take protesting—especially protesting something as important as a nuclear plant—too lightly. It's serious
business, and people can get hurt, just like they did in the
civil rights marches in the '50s and '60s, or the anti-Viet
Nam protests. Those people who understand the risks, and
feel that convinced and sincere about their stands should be
admired—even if you don't agree with them."

Ned twisted restlessly in his chair. "But to go out and beat
up people like that—and do you mean these people actually
went out there expecting to get beaten up?"

"No. I don't think they expected it. They probably had
been warned it could happen. But like most things and most
people, we don't believe it could ever happen here to us."

"Yeah. Well—it *did* happen. And where were the police?
Didn't they hear the rumors? Why didn't the plant guards
stop those men?"

His dad shook his head. "I can't answer those questions
nor do I want to if I could. I'm not trying to defend what
anyone did out there, just trying to explain the way it happens. The Niconda plant, as you know, is very important to
this town. A lot of people from town work out there. Store
owners depend on the plant payroll so the workers and their
families will come and buy their merchandise, or eat and
drink at their restaurants and bars. If the plant expands, it

means more income for the town, more taxes for better schools and streets, more homes built. A lot's at stake for a great number of people—and so they get very emotional, irrational, and angry with anyone who threatens their welfare."

"But why Mr. Abinson—why beat him up so badly?"

"Well, Ned, you yourself said that Mr. Hinders did not like the way he was treated in his visit to your class. That might be part of it. Probably, though, it was the fact that Mr. Abinson lives in Wilkenton. He's been here for a few years, is one of us, and, suddenly, he's turned on the town. He's become a traitor, as they see it, one who would sell out the town's welfare to these foreign protesters. Mr. Abinson must have known he was taking a chance when he decided to march with the protesters. They might have gone after him as a warning to anyone else who might decide to turn traitor in this town."

His dad got up from his chair, pushing the newspaper onto the floor. He walked over to the window and drew the curtains apart.

Ned stood up and turned toward his dad. "Do you mean if they had recognized me—Ned Turner—there, they might have marked me for a traitor and beaten me up, too?"

There was no answer from his dad.

Then his dad turned from the window and looked right at Ned. "Be careful, Ned, just be careful."

16

Morning came. The weekend had ended.

Kathy had called the night before to tell Ned she had arrived back from Spokane.

Ned hadn't told her anything about what had happened at the plant—even about Mr. Abinson. He just didn't want to relive or talk about it any more.

The only story the town's newspaper had about the beatings was a small article reporting that there was a protest out at the plant and things had gotten out of hand, with a few people from town and from the march "throwing some punches." That was it.

Ned met Kathy outside the physics room before class began. They smiled at each other and stood facing one another awkwardly.

"Three days hasn't changed you so much," Kathy teased. "You just look a little older—gray hairs around the tops of your ears."

"Oh, yeah! Well, sister, take this from a gray-haired junior, you're waddling more since last I saw you."

"Humpf!" Kathy flashed him a smile and dramatically walked into the room.

The bell rang for the start of the period.

Students settled in their seats, still talking. When Mr. Abinson would appear, then they would reduce their talking to low whispers.

Ned watched the door, hoping Mr. Abinson would walk in as if nothing had happened last Friday. He felt a little guilty. Maybe he should have called Mr. Abinson at home to see how he was. Ned had called the hospital and found out that Mr. Abinson wasn't admitted there as a patient. So, maybe he'd be back and wasn't hurt that much.

Over the whispers, Ned heard Jake's voice. "I bet he don't show for at least a week. I heard they really beat the stuffing out of him. Just whaled him! I'll give you five to one that he's out until next Monday at least. Any takers?"

Ned couldn't believe it when five boys got up and walked over to Jake's desk to place their bets with him. How could those guys do something like that—bet on how badly their teacher was beaten up!

Kathy had heard Jake also. "What happened to Mr. Abinson? What's all this about, Ned?"

Before Ned could answer, Jake leaned over to her and said, "Gone for a few days, Kathy girl, and you miss one of the most exciting episodes in the history of Wilkenton—the day that Mr. Abinson marched with the protesters, turned traitor to this town, and got the heck knocked out of him. Yes, Ma'am, quite a story—a physic-cal one. Get it?" Jake laughed at his pun. No one else did.

Kathy's eyes widened. "Do you mean they beat him up for that—just for marching in the protest?"

Both Ned and Jake nodded.

"That's awful . . . I don't think he should have gone with them like that—but to beat him up? That's not right."

"You want more details, girl?" said Jake. "Ask your lover-boy here. Old Ned was out in the desert taking in the whole scene. Why he even came home with that nice redhead in the tight jeans hanging on his arm."

Ned gasped for air.

Kathy looked at Ned closely. "You were—were there?"

Ned slowly nodded. "I was—there. Just out of curiosity—that's all. I was bored—you were gone—"

"And the cat must play!" cut in Jake.

Ned scowled at Jake and then turned back to Kathy. "I saw the whole thing—the men from town coming out, the way they attacked those poor people down there. I saw it from the hill. I saw them beating Mr. Abinson. I tried to help him—but couldn't . . . And then I heard Jane scream—"

"Jane?" Kathy's eyebrows arched.

"Yeah, well—uh—Jane screamed. So I pushed this guy off her and got her away. I couldn't just leave her there. Those guys might have really done something to her."

"Great story, Ned boy—just great! A real adventure tale." Jake giggled.

"You'll get the golden bandage for the first aid Volunteer of the Year award." Kathy didn't look at Ned. The words slid out of the corner of her mouth.

In through the doorway came a large man with glasses.

He looked confused and rushed. "Sorry, sorry. I didn't know I had this class, too. Sorry I'm late." His squeaky voice made Ned's ears want to shut the man out. Who could stand a whole period of that voice?

"I'm—I'm—I mean, I'll be your new teacher for a while, I guess. At least, that's what they told me. I told them I didn't know too much about physics or chemistry. I told them I was a biology person, but they wouldn't listen. They said that 'a science substitute is a science substitute. Do what you can.' So, I told them—I told them I would do what I could. . . ."

"Where's Mr. Abinson and when will he be back?" came a voice from the side of the room.

"Gone—he's gone. Mr. Abinson is gone," the man repeated.

"Yes, we can see that he's gone, but when will he—be—back—in—this—class?"

"I don't know. I don't know when he will be back—I don't know—"

17

Kathy had left school before Ned could meet her. She had walked home by herself.

Ned had kicked the locker four times in disgust. Why was she so burnt up? He'd only helped the girl. Couldn't Kathy understand that?

He took out some books, slammed the locker shut, and started walking home.

On the way home, he passed the street where Mr. Abinson lived with his family.

Ned paused and looked down the street.

He turned right and walked down the street toward the Abinson house.

When Ned reached the front of the white house with the red trim, he saw the debris and garbage that had been strewn across the lawn. The front windows—one a big picture window—were broken, and the white front door had a large splotch of black paint that had run from the top of the door to almost the bottom before drying.

Ned stared at the scene. . . . He hesitated—and then walked through the garbage to the front door. He knocked at the extreme right of the door to avoid the thick black paint.

He waited.

He knocked on the door again, more loudly.

"Go away! Leave us alone! Please leave us alone!" came a woman's hysterical voice.

Ned swallowed hard. "Mrs. Abinson? Is that you? . . . This is Ned Turner—Ned Turner, Mrs. Abinson."

"Go away!"

"I'd—I'd like to know how Mr. Abinson is? Is he all right? He wasn't in school today. . . ."

Someone shuffled slowly to the door.

The door opened.

There stood Mrs. Abinson, a thin woman, maybe two inches shorter than Ned's five feet, ten inches. She turned her face up to him. It was red, drawn, almost sickly in appearance.

"What do *you* want?"

Ned could see the pain and suffering in her face. What could he say to her—to Mr. Abinson? "I just—came by to—uh—see if Mr. Abinson was OK . . . It was rotten what they did to him—beating him like that. . . . I'm sorry."

She looked hard into his eyes. "Yes—they beat him—beat him good. But that was only the start of it. For the last two nights, once the word got around, they've been out here yelling, throwing garbage on the lawn, breaking our windows, hurling paint at the house. . . . When he went out to speak to them, they pushed him back inside and slammed the door in his face. . . . Oh, we called the police—the sheriff—and they came—two hours, three hours later—to fill out a report. They were just too busy to come when we needed them. . . . My children can't go outside. None of us can sleep."

She turned her back to Ned and shuffled back into the living room, leaving him standing in the open doorway.

A voice called, "Ned—Ned Turner, come on in, will you please? And shut the door."

Ned closed the door and followed the sound of the voice into the living room.

Mr. Abinson sat in a hard-wood chair with his leg propped up on a cushion. One of his eyes was black-and-blue, his upper lip looked swollen, and three fingers on his right hand were taped in a splint.

Ned stopped on the other side of the room. "I—I just wanted to know how you were." He looked at his teacher. His question seemed ridiculous with the way Mr. Abinson appeared—and with the way the house was.

"OK. I'll be OK. Don't worry. It's nice of you to be concerned. It's nice to know someone is still concerned."

"Mr. Abinson—I—I tried to stop them—when they were beating you. I tried . . . but I couldn't do much. It was insane—crazy—"

His teacher smiled a little. "I know, Ned. I remember seeing you for a moment when you knocked one of the men off me. I know you tried—and I'm grateful you cared."

His wife came back into the room. "Cared? You seem to be the *only* one who cares around here. The few friends we have here—they don't care. They don't call. They haven't offered to help. . . . You know, he doesn't have a job. He's not your teacher anymore. They fired him."

"You mean you won't be back at Wilkenton High? They fired you—just for marching?"

"Fired him! They even called a *special Sunday* meeting to fire him. That Mr. McDuffy, one of the big vice presidents of Niconda and head of the school board, he called the meeting—an emergency meeting. They just phoned us Sunday night to tell us. They said it was in the best interests of the students and the community . . . that's what they said."

She slumped down into a chair in a corner of the room.

Mr. Abinson stared out the window while his wife rambled on and on about what had happened to them since the march.

"What did my husband do that was so wrong? I'll tell you what he did: he voiced his opinion; he stated his concerns. He was afraid of nuclear power and what it could do to all of us. He was a man of conscience—and now," she laughed bitterly, "he is a man with no job and no friends."

Ned's knees felt weak. He wanted to sit down—but he also wanted to leave as soon as he could.

When his wife had stopped, Mr. Abinson said, "Sit down for a moment, will you, Ned?"

Ned sat down on the edge of the couch.

"Ned, what I did, I did because I believed it was right— one of the only ways to show that I have some serious concerns about nuclear power, and about that plant being here in this town. There's nothing bad about demonstrating peacefully, showing your concerns openly and hopefully convincing others to join you. Our country has a long history of

106

demonstrating against and for things in which we believe. But that doesn't mean that everyone is going to like what you're doing—or even want you to do it. I knew there would be some bad feelings once I went on that march. Maybe I was a little naïve not to see how much bad feeling there would be—and the pressures I would put on my family."

Ned listened. He wanted to understand.

"So, I did what I thought was right. . . . Just because you follow what you believe in doesn't mean that everything will turn out OK all the time. You understand? But we all must make choices—do what we think is best or true to ourselves—and then, I guess, live with the results of those choices. In this case, the results meant a sound beating, losing my job, and being branded an outcast. . . . It's hard to swallow."

Ned interlocked his fingers and pressed them hard together to drain some of the emotions welling up inside himself.

"But I don't want you to go, Mr. Abinson. I'm not so sure I understand—or believe in what you did—but I really don't want you to go. You're a pretty good teacher, you know?"

Mr. Abinson shifted his leg slightly on the cushion. He winced in pain. "I—I appreciate that, Ned. It's nice to hear—especially now. But I'm afraid my teaching days at Wilkenton High are over—and so is my stay in this town. The only thing I can do now is pack up my family, sell this house, and leave—to look for another teaching job somewhere else."

Ned nodded. He stood up to go. There was nothing he could do here. But he wanted to ask, Why you, Mr. Abinson? Why not someone else I didn't like so much—someone who wasn't such a good teacher, such a nice person? Why?

"Before you go, Ned, I have something here you might want to read sometime—hopefully soon." He reached down to the floor with his good hand and brought up two hardback books. "This is where I got the information I was referring to in class, about the nuclear accident near Detroit. True, these books are against nuclear power—but read them, for me. See what they have to say. Read some other things, too—in newspapers, magazines, and other books. Then make your own decision about this issue."

Ned took the books and nodded. The last thing he felt like doing now was sitting down and reading books.

"Good-bye, Ned—and thanks again for coming here. That took some courage."

The blood felt drained from Ned's face.

He looked once more at Mr. Abinson, then went to the doorway of the living room. He half-turned around and whispered "Good-bye" to his teacher . . . and then left the house.

18

At two o'clock Thursday morning, in pitch blackness, the sirens screamed.

Ned snapped upright in bed, trying to clear the sleep from his mind.

At first, he thought, "Fire!" But he smelled nothing, and the sound wasn't that of fire engines.

Then, he knew—and somehow he knew that this was no siren test, not this time. There had never been a siren test at this time of the morning. Even the federal government wouldn't do something like that! This time those screaming sirens meant the real thing—a nuclear accident at the plant . . . Ned knew it. A coldness went through him.

George started yelling and crying from the next room.

Ned got out of bed, tripped over something in the dark, and hurried to George's room. In the darkness, he couldn't make out where George was.

For some reason, Ned didn't want to turn on the light.

He followed the sounds of the crying to the closet. There,

surrounded by shoes and shoe boxes and under hanging clothes, huddled little George.

Ned bent down and gathered his young brother in his arms. He lifted George out of the shoes and shoe boxes, and took him over to the bed.

The sirens still kept screaming.

George covered his tiny ears with his hands, but he couldn't shut out the sound.

Ned held him, held George against his chest.

By this time, his parents, whose bedroom was at the other end of the house, came running to George's room.

"Everyone OK here?" his dad asked as he tied the sash on his robe. His mom stood to take George into her arms.

"It's all right, George. It will be quiet soon. In just a few minutes, it will be quiet again," she said to him.

But the sirens did not stop.

As the screaming sound continued to slice through the night, Ned could see the tension build in his dad. His dad was worried—very worried.

"Why don't we all go down to the living room and stay together for a while. Maybe the radio will tell us what's happening," suggested his dad.

They all got up and walked out of the room.

The four of them started down the stairs.

Then, the loudspeaker bullhorns started rolling through the streets of Wilkenton. "Please remain calm. You are to stay in your houses. Do not use the telephones unless it is an absolute emergency. Your cooperation is needed . . . Please remain calm . . ."

The voice droned on as it passed down the street repeat-

110

ing its message. At night, in the dark like this, it seemed as if alien monsters had just captured the town. The voice was eerie—scary. Ned shivered. He could look outside, but he couldn't see what might be happening out there to Kathy, to his friends, to the town.

In the living room, they turned on the radio. No TV this time of night.

Nothing. Just late night mood music—for lovers.

They switched to the other two stations.

Nothing. Just more mood music. Maybe the disc jockeys were asleep. Maybe they couldn't hear the sirens blaring in their soundproof control room booths. Maybe they weren't even alive anymore?

George fell asleep in his mother's arms. Ned slumped back on the couch.

Ten minutes—twenty minutes—forty minutes passed. The mood music continued to flow uninterruptedly from the radio.

The sirens had stopped some time ago. The loud bullhorns had passed and disappeared into the night. Outside it was deathly still. Even the crickets had stopped their racket.

Then, finally, "We interrupt the scheduled programming for a special emergency bulletin. We have been notified by the officials at the Niconda Nuclear Plant that there has been a minor incident at the plant. There is the possibility of some small leakage of radioactive materials into the atmosphere around the locale of the plant—a temporary condition. Officials ask that, until further notice, every person in the vicinity of the town of Wilkenton and within a five-mile radius of town stay near your homes so you may hear the latest bulletins and be contacted if necessary. The electricity in homes may be used, but usage should be kept to a minimum. . . . We will now repeat the bulletin from the Niconda Nuclear Plant . . . We have been notifi . . ."

Ned and his parents sat in silence listening to the bulletin repeated over and over again.

As it was being read for the fifth time, Ned's dad got up and switched off the radio. He then walked to the window and looked out at the dark, lamplit street.

Dad turned and walked to the phone. He picked up the phone and dialed. Ned could hear a busy signal sound. His dad dialed again—still the same beeping tone.

Hanging up the receiver, his dad turned to them and smiled. "Looks like we're all indoors for a while, girl and boys." But his smile didn't have its usual lightness. "In the morning we should break out the Monopoly game from dustballs and see how warped the Ping-Pong table is. But right now there's nothing we can do. I can't get through to the plant to find out anything more. So let's try to get back to sleep."

George had already fallen sound asleep.

For what seemed like the whole rest of the night, Ned lay in his bed unable to sleep. Too many things ran through his head. He had dreams when he closed his eyes—all sorts of dreams. He saw Mr. Abinson lying on the ground screaming, "Watch out! Watch out! It'll get you. Run!" And Ned would run and run and run.

Other dreams were about explosions. He'd see the plant explode and people—people he knew—and cars and houses go flying in all directions. He'd race to Kathy's house and find her lying there on the floor—dead. In another dream about an explosion, he would return to Wilkenton after everyone and everything had been destroyed. He would wander the desert, crossing the hill near the plant. There, in a piece of sagebrush, he would see his handkerchief. He'd pick it up, and feel it. It would be wet—wet from tears—Jane's tears. He would hear her voice across the desert, "I wish they had listened. I wish they could have known. Now everything's gone—gone—gone . . ."

With each dream, Ned would wake up in a cold sweat. Several times his stomach cramped severely. The thoughts ran through his head, "I've got it—radiation poisoning. I'm dying. It's destroying my insides. Kathy will never see me again. I have to explain—explain to her about Jane. She doesn't understand. . . ." but the phone would be dead.

Ned got out of bed and went to sit in the cushioned chair next to his bedroom window.

He looked down at the street. Nothing. No one moved—no cars—not even the yowling of cats on a fence. True, it was four in the morning and not much was ever happening at four in the morning, but usually, something moved—a truck, cows mooing on the distant farms, screeching birds. Gee! Had even the birds closed themselves up in their nests when the sirens went off? Maybe the birds had all organized and built lead-lined nests with matching covers, big enough for ten bird families. It could be. Animals are a lot smarter than people! And don't get their worlds in half as much trouble!

The sickening thing about this, though, was not knowing. If there was a fire—a gigantic fire with flames shooting

113

hundreds of feet in the air—at least, you could see it, feel it, know the damage it was doing and try to fight the fire. Or, if there was a tidal wave—one that you could see rising in the sky ready to crash down on the town—you knew what was coming. (Ned smiled to himself at the thought of a tidal wave in the desert.) But with this radiation thing—what was it? You couldn't see it—not unless there was a tremendous explosion or something. You couldn't be sure you felt it, but all the time it could be in the air, on the ground, in your body eating away at you and every living thing around you. . . . Did his dad or his mom have it? What about little George? Kathy?

Ned pushed himself up from the chair. He felt weak, dizzy.

He walked to the bathroom, closed the door, and let the shower run—hard. Taking his clothes off, he climbed into the shooting streams of water. A good scrubbing might help cleanse things.

While under the water, he had a picture in his mind of Jake—smiling. Jake had won the bet on the sirens.

19

The next morning everyone was down for breakfast by six, even though they had nowhere to go.

Red-eyed, worried, but trying to be cheerful, they were, ironically, together as a family for breakfast for one of the few times during the year. Usually, Dad went to work in his study or downtown to his law office. Mom had to change George or get him washed up. Ned, most often, ran late and grabbed some juice, milk, and a banana on the way out the door to school.

Now they sat, eating silently, looking at each other, giving one another that brief "everything's-going-to-be-all-right" smile. Even George stopped his squirming for a while.

It seemed like low-hanging, dark clouds had somehow gotten into the house, despite the doors and windows being closed. The clouds fogged the vision. You could see each other OK, but you weren't too certain that whom you were looking at was really there. This whole night and morning didn't seem real to Ned—not real at all.

The radio played fast-paced, cheery songs, while they all listened and waited for the next news bulletin. The bright music only made everything seem worse. The music seemed wrong for whatever was happening to them, to their town.

Ned drank some coffee—but it didn't help much.

The phone rang in the living room.

The sound jarred everyone at the table. They looked toward the other room, but no one wanted to get up from the table to answer the ringing phone.

The ringing seemed to grow louder and louder.

Finally, Mom pushed her chair away from the table. With a deep sigh, she got up and walked to the living room.

The phone stopped its incessant ringing.

"Hello?" she said. "Jack—Jack—it's for you. The phone call is for you, Jack."

Dad went to answer it.

Mom retreated back to the kitchen table with her sons.

"Yes? This is Jack Turner—yes—I am the State Representative from here. Washington, D.C., calling? . . . Hello, Senator . . . We're fine here so far. Do you know what's going on? . . . I see—emergency . . . the hot crew is there? Do you really think that might be necessary, Senator? It might cause more panic . . . Investigation? Certainly, I expect that the NRC and some government people would investigate, Senator. The people would expect it. . . . You want me to form this citizens' committee right after this accident—excuse me, incident—is over. You want me and this committee to explain what happened at the plant—to tell the people that everything is under control. But *is* it under control?"

The half-conversation continued for almost twenty minutes. Ned tried to glue the missing half together with his dad's comments and replies. Hot crew? Emergency? Panic? Investigation? Nothing Ned heard made him feel any better about what was going on outside.

". . . but, Senator, you can't expect . . . I'm new to this public committee—a few weeks . . . I have no information. I have little knowledge or experience with nuclear power and its problems. How can I head this committee now? . . . I realize that I'm here and no one else is nearby, but I don't have the information yet. You never sent me the main part of the material. I was supposed to receive a complete portfolio on the background information, studies, and current concerns. Where is it? . . . You didn't think there was any reason to rush the material to me? . . . It's there on your desk? You'll send it by special mail today? . . . I certainly hope you do."

Ned could see that this phone call from the Senator had rattled his dad badly. Ned knew his dad only got rattled like this when someone put him in a position he didn't want to be in—when he got shoved into something he knew nothing about. Especially, something like this. Dad was just lousy in physics and chemistry.

". . . So, how am I supposed to handle all this? Who else will be here? You'll send government experts—scientists. Well, that will help . . . Besides, what? . . . a good political move? . . . This isn't something I'd planned to boost my political image, Senator. I can think of better ways to do that than have a nuclear disaster—oh, incident, excuse me again. . . . You don't want to hear the words 'nuclear disaster'?

Isn't that what we're facing here? . . . Well, good-bye, Senator." The phone fell back onto its cradle. It severed the ties with Washington, D.C.

Ned walked to the living room doorway.

His dad sat slumped on the couch, head in his hands.

Ned joked, "You going to run for Senator, Dad?"

His dad looked up with a somber face. "Not if people like that can end up being Senators," he said, nodding toward the phone.

"What's happening, Dad? What do they want you to do? How bad is it at the plant?"

George and his mom had come into the room also.

Dad stood up as if he were about to deliver a lecture or make a speech. "Get this, will you? That was Senator Falconery on the phone. He wants me to get this citizens' committee together to inform the people about concerns, problems, whatever at the nuclear plant, now that this accident has happened. Well, this thing that happened at the plant is pretty serious. It started about ten hours before they decided to sound those sirens. They had thought they could stop it. Water—there's some radioactive water leaking in the containment building and some outside vent is stuck. Anyhow, from what I could understand from the Senator, radioactive gases are leaking. . . . He didn't seem that clear on what it was all about . . . His main concern was that the national media would have a field day with this. And the Senator's probably right. They'll blow this thing way out of proportion."

"But I thought, Dad, that they had all these safety systems

and checks, and trained people. That's what Mr. Hinders said. He said it couldn't happen."

"Looks like it did happen, Ned."

No one said a word for a moment.

"They may have to evacuate." His dad didn't look at any one of them.

"What, Jack?"

Dad cleared his throat. "If they can't stop the leak or if it should get worse, they'll call for a general evacuation of everyone in the area, a five- or ten-mile radius of the plant."

His mom's eyes widened in alarm. "But when will they know? What's to happen to everything, Jack? What do we do until then?"

Before answering, his dad tightened his fists. "Until we know what's happening—until they give us some signal—we have to remain around the house. At least they'll be able to contact me here and we can find out what's happening."

"But, Jack, how long can we—or any of us—stay around the house?"

"We can do it—for a while, Barb. We need to plan out how to use what food we have. We're probably only talking about two days or so. They'll either have to come to some decision to evacuate by then or decide that the danger has passed. Otherwise, there will be panic—and people will start doing very stupid things."

Ned reached down and picked up George. "OK, George, let's get organized!"

That broke the tension. Dad took out a note pad and pencil. "Time to make lists: food, drink, things to do inside to

119

keep from going crazy. That last title took up the whole page!"

"Jack, can we drink the water? Wouldn't that be contaminated too?" asked Mom.

His dad paused, tapped his pencil on the pad in thought. "I don't know. As an uninformed member of the citizens' committee (not yet even formed) favoring nuclear power, I couldn't say officially. I couldn't say unofficially either."

"Well, then," added Mom, "let's turn on the TV and see if there are any reports. It's after seven now. Something should be on." She walked over to the TV and twisted the knob to "On."

A newscaster on the local TV station for the Wilkenton area was reading a report: ". . . people have been asked to remain in their homes until further notice. There is no need for undue concern. The officials at the Niconda Nuclear Plant state that everything is under control—and that special technicians have been flown in to help correct the problem. . . . We have with us in our studio a Mr. Ralph Jackson, public relations director for the Niconda plant. He will explain what has happened at the plant and what is being done there. Mr. Jackson."

Dad, Mom, and Ned sat down to listen. George crawled under the coffee table.

The TV cameras panned across to a broad-shouldered, six-foot man in his fifties. He spoke in a deep voice. "Thank you. I have been asked to appear on this TV station in order to reassure you that the present incident we have at the plant is under control. We have the utmost concern for the health and welfare of the people in Wilkenton and elsewhere near the plant. So, on the very slight chance that any escaping radiation—despite its extremely low level—should affect any person, we ask that you remain in your homes for emergency instructions until the problem is definitely solved."

The newscaster asked, "Mr. Jackson, what exactly happened at the Niconda plant early this morning?"

"Well, I will try to explain it in layman's terms. It seems a pipe near the reactor, inside the containment building, began leaking water. It was too close to the reactor to shut it off with a valve. Now, we have considered the problem and planned as our strategy to still pump water through that pipe to keep the reactor as cool as possible. In the meantime, we are shutting down the reactor itself. All seems under control. There is no cause for undue alarm. And, let me repeat, there is no possibility—none whatsoever—of any type of explosion occurring from this pipe break within the reactor building itself."

"But, Mr. Jackson, there have been reports of gases—radioactive gases—leaking into the air."

"Yes. Well, there are, at times, some minute quantities of gases being released. We must do this to prevent a pressure build-up in the containment building itself. But the amount of gases emitted are at such a small level that there is no danger to man nor beast."

"So you say, Mr. Jackson, that there is no cause for any alarm?"

Ned had the distinct feeling that this man's broad, beaming smile had been taped on his face just for this show. Maybe they had jammed foot-long toothpicks on the insides of his cheek pouches. The more Ned watched that smile, the less he heard the man's words—or believed what he was saying.

"There is simply no need for alarm. As I said, this is a minor incident and it is under control. The amount of radiation that is entering the atmosphere equals about as much as you would receive from an X ray at your doctor's. That's all—the amount of an X ray."

"The amount of an X ray," his dad repeated out loud. "There's only one problem with that explanation. A doctor's X ray takes a few seconds—and it's over. Who knows how long we may be exposed to radiation and radioactive particles? Who knows? . . . And why the sirens then, if there is no cause for concern and if they have everything under control? Why the sirens? Why is the Senator so concerned?"

Unfortunately, the newscaster didn't hear his dad's questions.

"But," continued the newscaster, "will there be any long-term effects on people?"

"We doubt it. There's no proof that there will be."

"Have there been any injuries at the plant, to the men working there?"

"No serious injuries at all. Some have felt a little nauseous—sick to their stomachs—but that will pass, the doctors say. One man fell against a hot pipe and received a slight burn. The workers at the plant now are staying there voluntarily to help out in any way they can. They will be perfectly OK. I realize that some families might be concerned about husbands or wives at the plant, but please don't try calling the plant itself because we need to keep our phone lines open. Everyone will be just fine—just fine." His pasted smile seemed to cast an eerie glow over the TV screen.

"Thank you, Mr. Jackson. We'll return periodically with updated bulletins about the incident at the Niconda Nuclear Plant. Now back to our regular programming."

Dad walked over and twisted the nob to "Off." He stood there looking at the blank screen.

"Well, what do you think, Dad?"

"We just got the official word," he said. "They told us it was only an 'incident'—a minor radiation matter."

"You don't exactly sound like you believe him, Jack. Do you?"

His dad tapped the top of the TV set with his fingers. "He doesn't overwhelm me with his honesty and expertise, Barb. I wouldn't bet he's telling the whole truth and nothing but, so help him God! How much of the truth he knows and is willing to tell is the prize question. He certainly didn't mention any hot crew coming out to help clean up, as the Senator did."

"So, what do we do now, Dad?" Ned felt afraid, but he didn't know exactly what he was afraid of—where to direct his fear. He hoped his dad would solve the problem—take the fear away.

"When the alert is over and we can travel outdoors, I'll be right at that plant to find out what was going on there. But until then, let's make out lists—as many lists as we can—and then do some of those things we haven't done in a long, long time together as a family."

"But, Jack, how long—how long can we stay in here?"

20

Night came.

Still the streets remained empty—no people, no cars, not even dogs chasing cats. Each family stayed—sealed—within its home, afraid of leaving the house.

TV and radio bulletins began to come more and more frequently, especially now that Niconda was receiving national news coverage. The bulletins told of Krypton gas, iodine particles, and Strontium-90 leaking out from the vent in the containment building. The newscaster had said that there were only small amounts leaking out—but still the gases *were* leaking.

To help lessen the frustration of not being able to do anything or really go anywhere, Ned and his dad played Monopoly most of the afternoon. Ned couldn't remember the last time he and his dad had just sat playing Monopoly. Father and son together—funny the things that brought them together like this.

Each person in the house talked as little as possible about the nuclear plant for the rest of that day. Every hour one of them would turn on the TV or radio to hear the latest news bulletin.

Four times during the afternoon Ned had tried to call Kathy. He was worried about her. He wanted to hear her voice—to know she was all right, to know that she had forgotten about that red-headed girl and the march, and that she loved him. But every time the line had been busy.

His dad had had one other call from D.C. He didn't say much about it. Ned had asked, but his dad waved him off with "nothing really new."

At a little after 9:00 P.M., Ned tried to phone Kathy again. This time he heard the ring at the other end of the line.

Someone answered the phone and anxiously asked, "Bert? Is that you, Bert? When will you be home?"

Ned knew it was Kathy's mother, and that she was hoping it was her husband calling. That meant that Kathy's dad was probably still at the plant.

"Mrs. Jenkins? This is Ned. Is Kathy there?"

She didn't answer immediately.

Ned felt strange holding the phone and waiting for her to realize that it wasn't her husband.

"Bert? Isn't this Bert?"

"No, Mrs. Jenkins. This is Ned Turner—Ned Turner. I wanted to speak to Kathy. Is everything OK there?"

No answer.

"Can I speak to Kathy, Mrs. Jenkins?"

Someone took the phone away from Mrs. Jenkins. "Hello? Who is this?"

"Kath? Kathy? Is that you? I wanted to know how you were—if everything was OK and—"

"Ned?"

"Is everything all right, Kath? Your mom sounded frightened or something."

"Yes. We're all right, Ned. Everything's fine." She forced her voice to sound cheerful. "It's just—well—mother is a little worried because my father is still not home. We guess—we think—he's still at the plant, but he probably hasn't been able to call us yet. We tried calling the plant, but the lines have been busy every time. Everybody's trying to call there now."

"I wouldn't worry, Kath. Tell your mother that the TV guy this morning said that the people at the plant were staying there to help out. That's all. Nothing to worry about."

"Do you think so, Ned? Do you really think so?" The cheerfully forced voice had broken. Ned could sense how worried Kathy was.

"I wish I could come over and be there with you, Kath."

"I do, too. It's lonely here. My mother doesn't want to do much except sit by the phone."

"Kath, that thing about the march and that girl—well—she—"

Suddenly, loud static cut into the phone line. An officious voice said, "Please keep this line free. We have limited service now."

Ned felt as if someone had been eavesdropping on their conversation. "Bye, Kath."

But the line was disconnected before she had a chance to say anything more to him.

Ned stood there holding the dead telephone in his hand. Slowly, he placed it back down on its base. "Weird," he thought. "That telephone and the TV are the only connections we have with the outside world. The mail hasn't come, no milk on the doorstep, no newspaper, no trips to the store for food—just the telephone and the TV. The TV you can't talk with and receive answers to your questions, and now the telephone you can't use to speak with people you love and are worried about. Isolation."

"I'm going to try to put George to sleep now. Say 'good night' to him, Ned," his mom said.

Ned took George in his arms and gave him a kiss on the cheek. George hugged Ned extra hard. Even George's hug felt more important today.

When they left to go upstairs, Ned sat down in a chair and thumbed through an old magazine. His dad had gone into the study and closed the door to be alone.

At eleven, Ned turned on the TV news.

". . . is still in effect for the Wilkenton area. The gas is still leaking from the dome area, although the amount of radiation leaking out has not significantly increased, according to nuclear scientists flown to the Niconda plant site. Some reports have filtered in about possible problems with the cooling system in the core reactor. No one at the plant would explain or confirm these reports. Another report said that the National Guard, with specially designed protective suits, could be called in to patrol the roads and streets if the alert continues. No serious injuries or casualties resulting from the accident at the plant have been reported to this station."

The waiting. The not knowing and the waiting. That's what really gets to you, Ned thought. What will happen to us? When will I see Kathy again? Will I see her again?

He didn't hear the rest of the news broadcast. The thoughts and worries kept repeating—echoing—inside his head over and over. . . . until, at last, he slumped back in the chair and fell asleep.

21

Early the next morning, the bullhorn trucks passed through the streets. "Please turn on your TV sets or radios and listen carefully to the latest bulletin from the Niconda plant . . . Please turn on . . ."

The four of them sat in front of the TV waiting for the harried newsman to collect himself and his information, and tell about the latest happenings at the plant.

"Good morning, ladies and gentlemen . . ."

The "Good morning, ladies and gentlemen" only seemed to make matters worse. Ned could see, by looking at the man's face, that *he* didn't think it was a good morning and that he didn't look like he had much to say that would be "good."

"The situation at the Niconda plant grew more serious during the night. Radioactive gases are still leaking into the atmosphere from a broken vent in the containment building. The rate of leakage has increased somewhat. In addition, all workers had to be cleared from the containment building where water is leaking from a broken valve onto the floor around the reactor. The water on the floor is highly radioactive—or what's called 'dirty water.'

"At this point, no one can enter the containment building to fix the valve. More and more dirty water pours onto the reactor floor. Water must be pumped into the reactor, even though leaking, to keep the core cool. The workers at Niconda are trying desperately to bring the reactor to a cold shut-down. But time is a factor.

"Some scientists, from what this reporter has learned, fear that if the pressure builds in the building and in the water pipe system to such an extent that it jams the pipes—and prevents water from cooling the reactor—there could be a disastrous melt-down. In order to reduce the pressure build-up inside the containment area, gases must be vented off. However, this has gotten out of control. The vent has jammed and the Niconda people cannot completely shut the vent to control the amount of emissions into the atmosphere. Experts have been carefully monitoring the degree of increasing radioactivity around the Niconda plant and surrounding area.

"For the public's own welfare, the governor of the State of Washington has strongly recommended that, for the time being, all pregnant women as well as children under five years old be evacuated from the contaminated areas near the plant. This is just a precautionary measure, but the radiation in the atmosphere might possibly cause some genetic damage to unborn children or to young children. Therefore, it seems best to the governor to evacuate these people from the danger area . . ."

Ned looked at his mom and George. What did this mean? They were going to take his mother and his brother away? Send them away from him and his dad?

". . . During the night, the National Guard was alerted. They have men and trucks that will arrive in Wilkenton by noon. The National Guard trucks will wait in the supermarket parking lot from 12 until 1:30. During that time, all pregnant women as well as mothers and their children five and under should meet at that location and board the trucks. The National Guard will transport them to the Red Cross facilities set up in Spokane. This evacuation may last several days or even a week. Please take any necessities with you, but only those items that are essential . . ."

Dad got up and put his arm around Mom's shoulder. "Let's go upstairs and get you both packed. You're taking a short vacation—and will have some nice fresh air and the outdoors to run around in."

"But I can't leave you—you and Ned—just like that, Jack. Who knows what could happen with that thing out there? It could explode. It might never stop leaking. I want to be with you . . . I want us together . . . I couldn't stand not knowing what's happening to you here." Mom drew back from following Dad.

Dad turned back to face her. "I know how worried you are—and how difficult it will be for all of us—when we're apart at a time like this. I'm worried and scared, too. But we can't let George stay here. We can't take that chance. And George needs you with him. We need you, too, Barb, but right now, George needs you more, I think. . . ." He tugged on her hand slightly. "Come on. Let's go up and pack some things. Besides, Barb, if they report any danger to the rest of the population, Ned and I will just climb in the car and drive away to meet you. We'll have the car here. We'll be OK."

Mom followed now, slowly ascending the stairs.

Ned sat staring at the figures on the TV screen. His mind felt numb. He heard words but didn't want to understand their meaning.

Most of the morning, his dad and mom spent packing clothes, toys, making sandwiches, planning what Ned and his dad would do around the house.

Ned hardly spoke to anyone. He spent the morning just sitting in the corner chair of the living room, looking outside at the silent street. He didn't want to talk—he didn't know what to say—to them, to his mother and brother. It felt like the end of the world was coming. Maybe some of those strange people had the right idea. Just sell everything, climb up to the top of a mountain, and wait there for the end of the world.

Even little George seemed unusually quiet—and cooperative—during the whole morning. He stayed up in his room playing with as many toys as he could—as if he were saying "good-bye" to them, to the ones he couldn't take with him. Maybe he knew—somehow—maybe he knew . . .

Trucks broke the sound of street silence. Heavy motors, thudding brakes, crunching massive tires moved down the streets.

Ned saw the trucks move past his house, down the street toward the supermarket's parking lot. He watched them warily, like they were some mechanical monsters sent by alien beings to invade Wilkenton.

Dad saw the trucks pass by too, and called out to everyone, "Let's get moving. Out to the car, everyone!"

Ned walked to the hallway. He hugged his mom and his brother.

Mom picked up a sack, and George clutched his stuffed gorilla. Dad led the way through the open front door carrying two large suitcases. Ned followed behind.

They all walked in single file to the car parked in the driveway. His dad opened the trunk and put the suitcases inside. Then they got into the car.

His dad backed the car out onto the street.

Ned noticed that his dad had not closed the garage door, but he didn't say anything about it. He could only think, They're being taken away—my mother and my brother—separated from us so easily, so suddenly. How could this happen? What was going on?

". . . before you know it, Barb, you and George will be back here with us. They'll clear this thing up in a short while. . . ."

Ned could see cars and people crowding into the parking lot. People shouting, some crying, others standing hugging each other, unable to speak their feelings.

His dad stopped the car alongside the street curb. They opened the doors and got out. Ned held George's small hand. Opening the trunk, Dad lifted out both suitcases. Mom filled her arms with the stuffed gorilla and carry-on things they had for the trip.

"Barbara, this is just a precautionary measure, they said. If they thought the danger was that serious, they'd evacuate everyone in the area—not just pregnant women and young children. We'll be fine. We'll even clean the house for you. Won't we, Ned?"

Ned tried to smile, but couldn't. His eyes focused on the ground. "Sure—sure, Dad."

"That doesn't make me feel any better, Jack. Every time you've cleaned the house—it looked worse!" His mom laughed, but a few tears ran down her cheek.

"They're waiting for us, Barb." He helped Mom up into the truck. Some fifteen or twenty other women and young children were already sitting inside on the wooden benches.

Next, his dad passed George up into the truck. George grabbed his stuffed gorilla and clutched it to his small chest.

Mom leaned down from the truck to give Dad and Ned one last kiss. Then she walked back into the dark shadows of the truck and sat down on a bench. George climbed into her lap.

The truck gears groaned and shifted. The truck started moving down the street—away from them.

Dad and Ned waved, but, in the dark shadows, they couldn't tell if Mom and George waved back.

He and his dad watched the truck disappear from sight. Even with all the other people around them, Ned felt that he and his dad were alone.

They drove home to a silent house.

As soon as he passed through the front door of their family home, Ned felt the cold emptiness of the house. It wasn't a home any longer—it was just a house.

22

At 1:00 P.M., the TV news reported that some 170 people had left the area in the National Guard trucks and were now settled in the emergency Red Cross center in the high school gym in Specter Creek on the outskirts of Spokane.

An hour later, the bullhorn trucks set off again on their rounds of the streets. "Please listen carefully. We realize that for many of you food may be a problem. We do not want you to be out on the streets for extended periods of time. That is why the mayor closed stores, schools, and public buildings, so people would remain close to their homes. Food, however, will be available at grocery stores for a short period of time.

"The mayor has ordered that all grocery stores be open from 3:00 until 5:00 P.M. today so that you may purchase food for your families. The stores will *only* be open during these times. The National Guard will help supervise conduct in the stores . . . We repeat. Please . . ."

"What does the mayor think he's doing?" his dad stormed,

after hearing the bulletin. "He's going to cause a panic—a big stampede. It's crazy!"

Ned's dad walked quickly to the phone and dialed. He waited impatiently for someone to answer the phone on the other end.

"Hello? . . . Hal? This is Jack Turner. Look—I just heard that bulletin about opening the grocery stores for two hours and then clearing the streets again. Hal, that's going to cause a mess. People will panic. They'll be going crazy to grab all the food they can—

"OK—so the truck drivers maybe won't haul food down here when there's this alert and the area may be contaminated, but is this the only way to do it? Why not space things out somehow? Let different sections of the town come to the store at different times?

"I know, Hal. I know we don't know how long this thing could last—or if it will end. Certainly, I'm worried, too, but . . .

"I don't think it's a good choice, Hal, but for your sake and for the sake of the people of Wilkenton, I hope it works out. Good-bye."

His dad hung up the phone, drummed his fingers on top of the receiver, and then did an abrupt about-face to Ned.

"Ned, make a list of what we need. We'll stock up. This may be the only trip we get to the store for a while, so make it a good list. We have an hour to get to the grocery." Dad walked to the kitchen, piled the dishes in the sink, and went to change his clothes.

Just the thought of getting out—of going into town to shop—made Ned feel better. He didn't even think of any possible radiation dangers outside. The sun was shining. It looked fine out.

Fifteen minutes later, they both got into the car.

Cars seemed to appear from everywhere. Traffic jammed up long before they got to Main Street. Cars, vans, trucks were bumper-to-bumper. Drivers honked incessantly—leaned their heads out the window to yell angrily at the driver in front of them. Anger, frustration, desperation sounded in their voices. Each one had to reach the grocery store, shop, and return home before the 5:00 P.M. curfew.

"What are we going to do, Dad? We just turned on to Main, but if we sit here in line like this and then spend more time trying to find a place to park, it'll take way over an hour. We won't get any food—even if there was anything left to buy."

Dad drummed his fingers on the steering wheel, shooting glances to his left and right, cursing when he looked straight ahead at the traffic.

It was a warm mid-fall day, in the 70s. But Ned saw that as hot as it was most people had their car windows open only a crack. They must have felt safer from the radiation that way.

His dad slammed on the brakes to avoid hitting the car in front.

"OK. You're right. If we keep this up, we get no food to take home."

"So? What do you think, Dad?"

"Well, I'm stuck here in the car. We can't move forward and we can't move back. Only thing I can think of is that you walk to the store. It's only about three blocks more or so. If you can get a shopping cart, buy things we need and wheel the cart back until you see me. We can do it. What do you say?"

Ned looked out the window as if he were trying to see something in the air outside. "Yeah. Sounds like the only way, Dad. I'm game for going."

Dad let go of the steering wheel with his right hand and reached in his back pocket. He took out his wallet. "Here's $40. That should do it. And be careful. People are liable to be very edgy—panicky—you know, maybe do some strange things in this type of situation. So, Ned, be alert and take care."

"I will, Dad. You, too. . . . See you soon." Ned looked back over at his dad. Then he opened the car door, stepped out on the sidewalk, and quickly slammed the door shut.

It felt muggy—that's all. He didn't feel anything strange happening to him. He bent down to look inside the car, smiled and waved at his dad.

Walking down the street, he tried to test his physical reactions. Was anything changing? Could he feel something happening to his body? No, he didn't think so.

But, now, the thought struck him that he was alone. His mom and George had left in the truck, his dad sat alone in the car, and he, Ned, was out here alone in the middle of some invisible menace.

Other people rushed by him. Some he knew, but they didn't stop to say "hello."

Ned picked up his pace and moved even more quickly, weaving in and out of people walking more slowly than he.

He saw people sitting in their hot, humid cars. Some

138

looked angry, others stifled by the heat. Some looked just plain frightened, gripping the steering wheel with white fingers.

As he reached the front of the store, he saw people pushing and shoving to get in and out. Two National Guardsmen at each entrance tried to clear passageways for people to enter and leave the grocery store, but the number of people and their frantic efforts to get food overwhelmed the Guardsmen.

Most of the shopping carts had been swept away with the tides of people surging down the aisles stocked with food. People tried to line up at the check-out counters to pay for their groceries, but the shoving, bumping, hurrying people made it very difficult to stand in any sort of line for long.

Off in a corner of the store, near the coffee and tea, was a cart. Ned ran for it. He could hear several feet pounding behind him. He reached the cart and swung it to the right down a narrow path between the shelves. An older man and a middle-aged woman looked disgustedly and angrily after him. If they had all reached the cart at the same time, it would have been some battle—and Ned would probably have lost.

The cart certainly wasn't any prize. Two wheels didn't turn. So Ned had to shove it and slide it along.

Ned quickly got the idea that if you shopped with care to choose the best quality item at the best price, you'd end up with little or nothing to eat. Men, women, kids he went to school with moved rapidly down the aisles. Their arms reached out and grabbed cans of this, packages of that, bottles, cartons, sacks. It didn't seem to matter. They couldn't know exactly what they had. They just wanted to make sure they had something—something to feed themselves and their families.

Ned snatched packages of noodles and spaghetti. He took some bags and tossed in apples, bananas, oranges, celery, lettuce—without even examining how ripe they were. Someone bumped into him. The first thing Ned did was check to see that his food money had not been pick-pocketed. Then he threw several cans of fruits and vegetables into the cart.

At the end of the aisle, a woman yelled out as a cart careened around the corner and slammed into her leg. The person pushing the cart didn't even stop. A man passed by a young woman's cart and scooped out some food and dumped it in his own cart. The woman screamed and yelled for help—but none came, and the man sped away.

As he turned down the cereal aisle, Ned saw Kathy at the other end. He threw a box of Cheerios and one of Kix into his cart, and wheeled down the aisle toward her.

Before he reached her, a short, fat man pushed his cart so close to her that he smashed Kathy into the shelves. She fell down, holding her arm. The man paused for a second. "Watch out. Don't sit there. Move out of the way." And he kept going past her, leaving her there.

Ned helped her up. "Are you OK?" Her arm seemed bruised some, but otherwise all right.

"Ned, watch your cart!" Kathy yelled. A large woman was about to steal some of his canned food.

Ned leaped for the cart and pulled it back, right out from under her hand. She scowled and moved on.

"What are you doing here by yourself, Kathy? Why isn't your mom here to help?"

"She couldn't deal with this, Ned. She's in bad enough shape just waiting for a phone call from my father. She won't leave that phone. She sits there all day and most of the night waiting—waiting for a call from him. No call has come yet. We still can't get through to the plant. . . . I knew we needed food. So I came alone—walked here."

"Your arm's OK?"

"Yes—Ned! My food—my cart! Stop him!"

A boy of about fifteen had started pushing Kathy's cart away.

Ned grabbed him by the shirt collar and hauled him away from the cart. He flung the boy down on the floor. The boy scrambled to his feet, and fled down the aisle.

"Kathy, let's go. This place is crazy—the people are crazy! Let's pay for the food and get out of here. We only have thirty minutes left before they close the town down again. Hurry."

Ned led the way. Kathy followed him, trying to push the cart with one arm.

They waited in line—and waited—and waited.

The frantic grocery clerk tried to rush as much as possible and still collect the right amount of money for the food.

Fifteen minutes went by.

The people in the store grew more restless, more violent, more frantic to get their food and go home. The deadline for closing the store and getting off the streets was coming near.

Ned and Kathy finally reached the counter. What they

had forgotten about was that the carts had to remain in the store now. No one was allowed to take them out to a car for unloading groceries because the carts were needed by other people shopping. They had five sacks between them—five sacks of groceries. There was no way that they could carry all those sacks down the street to wherever Ned's dad might be—especially if they had to protect themselves and their food.

The clerk pushed their five sacks to the end of the counter, and rushed back to total up the next customer's bill.

"Stay here." Ned told Kathy.

Racing to his left, he took hold of a cart handle and almost flipped it over turning it around. He ran with it to the end of the counter and dropped all the sacks into the cart.

"Keep your hands on top, so things don't bounce out," he said to Kathy. "Let's go."

The two Guardsmen had their backs to them as they approached the exit door. They were watching the noise and people on the street.

"Now!" Ned yelled. He thrust the cart through the doorway between the surprised Guardsmen.

He and Kathy ran with the cart in front of them. She tried to keep her hand on the food, so it wouldn't fall out.

The two Guardsmen reached out to stop them, but they had been caught off-guard. They missed the cart, but one of them caught Kathy's blouse sleeve and ripped it. The Guardsmen yelled at them, but didn't give chase.

Ned bumped and raced back up Main Street searching for his dad's car in the still-clogged line of traffic. Ned hoped he could find him quickly, hoped he was still in the line. If not, they'd never make it back home.

Kathy tried her best to run alongside and keep her hands on top of the sacks of groceries.

Two vegetable cans and some bananas fell from the cart. Kathy stopped to pick them up.

"Don't stop for them, Kath. No time." She ran on with Ned.

In the moment the cans and bananas dropped to the sidewalk, hands scooped the food up and ran with it across the street. . . . Ned got a glimpse of a thin girl, about ten years old, running with the cans and bananas clutched to her chest.

Ned pushed the cart along. Kathy tried to smother the top of the cart with her body to keep the precious food in the basket when Ned wheeled the cart down and up curbs.

A horn honked. It honked again more loudly—in three short blasts.

Ned shot a look to the side. It was his dad, still stuck in the traffic line.

Ned swerved the cart toward the car.

His dad swung the back door open.

Kathy and Ned threw the sacks of groceries and spilled food into the back seat, and climbed in after, trying not to sit on the oranges.

"Close call, Dad. They're going nuts in there—just crazy!"

"Looks that way." His dad turned the car off into a side street and away from the congestion and noise.

"We'll take you home, Kathy. We only have five or ten

minutes before they start clearing the streets." Dad drove as fast as he could through the side streets, staying off the main roads.

In a few minutes, they pulled up in front of Kathy's house. Her mother was waiting at the window, staring out with tired, frightened eyes.

Ned and Kathy hurriedly sorted some of the groceries out and put them back into the sacks. Then Ned helped Kathy carry the sacks to her house.

Kathy's mother opened the door and took the sacks from Ned's arms.

"Oh! Thank you, Ned—thank you. Thank you for bringing my girl home safely . . . But you must hurry back home— quickly—the TV said you have only four minutes. You must hurry."

Ned didn't know how to react to Mrs. Jenkins' panic and fear.

He touched Kathy's arm as she entered the house. She turned. He leaned forward and kissed her lightly on the lips. Her eyes moistened.

Then he ran back to the car, climbed in, and he and his dad raced back to their home.

The two hours of release time—time out of their cage— had ended. The streets had to be cleared immediately. Within a half hour after the deadline, not a car or truck or person could be seen on the streets of Wilkenton.

Once more all outside was quiet—still—empty, and the people waited inside their homes.

23

That night the phone rang. It was the first time the whole day the phone had rung.

Mom had called.

"Barb? How are you? Where are you—in a gym?"

Ned went upstairs to listen on the extension phone.

"We're fine, Jack. Lonely, but fine. We're in the high school gym—yes. Each family has an army cot per person to sleep on. You know, I haven't slept on a cot since Girl Scout camp nearly thirty years ago! George likes it and took his nap right on it with no problem. We have a cardboard carton for some toilet articles and live out of the suitcases under the cot. Not much privacy—let me tell you that! Not too quiet either. Every kid crying and mothers screaming make echoes through the gym that bounce back at you from all four walls!" She laughed a little. She tried to make it all sound like some great adventure.

"Mom, it's really quiet here without you two. We got

some food today—but it was a mess in the store. People running, pushing, grabbing food."

"Sounds like I missed all the fun, Ned. I'd bet you bought every cookie in the place!"

"That's what I forgot to get!"

"Jack—Jack, have you heard anything more? Do they know when we can come home?"

"Not a word, Barb. I tried phoning D.C. several times this afternoon and evening, but I keep receiving this recording that all lines outside of the town are busy and reserved for emergency use only. They could call in, I'm sure. But if D.C. hasn't called me yet, well—I guess—well, I guess maybe they don't know, or can't take the time to explain, what's happening right now. So, we'll all just have to sit here a while and wait. I'm only down three games of Monopoly to my oldest son here—but he has yet to beat me in gin rummy!"

"Yeah, Mom, I'm not that far behind him in gin rummy. . . . Who knows? I may even start to read a book or two. Would you believe that?"

With a mock serious tone, she answered, "It takes something like this—a nuclear accident—to get you to read more? Well, at least, we can tell your teachers how to motivate you to read."

Ned heard some noises in the background. His mom wasn't on the phone anymore.

"Here's George," she finally said. "He wanted to say 'Hi' and then we have to hang up. There's a long line of people waiting to call home, too."

The phone on the other end changed hands with a good

deal of banging and scraping that jarred Ned's ear.

"George? George? This is your dad, George."

A few moments of silence—and heavy breathing on the other end of the line.

"Hi, Daddy. Hi, Ned." The receiver slammed down. The buzz reported the end of the telephone call.

Well, thought Ned, George never was much of a conversationalist. He came back downstairs.

"They sound like they're doing OK, don't they, Dad? Should have asked if they had seen my red-headed friend." Ned half-laughed when he mentioned her.

"They sound fine. But the house sure is empty without them. Funny, how you complain about the noise all the time, and when they're gone, you complain about the silence and quiet. Shows how hard it is to please people. Guess I should know that—I'm a politician." Dad sat down on the couch.

"Wonder how guys stand it behind bars—you know, being locked up in prison for years like that. Here we are just locked inside our house for a few days and we're going crazy just being inside a whole house! How do prisoners live through it all those years? What do they do with themselves? What do they think? I never want to find out firsthand. Let me tell you—never!" Ned paced in front of the couch.

"It must be rough, Ned. I hope neither one of us ever finds out what it's like. This is enough. The separation from your mother and George—the house confinement—the fear and uncertainty we have now is enough to feel and live through for just a few days."

Ned stopped and looked closely at his dad.

"You afraid, Dad?"

His dad took a deep breath and nodded. "Very much so, Ned. Yes, I'm afraid."

"I mean, are you really afraid—afraid for you?"

"I'm afraid for all of us—for what might happen to you and George and your mother—and for me, too. I don't want to end up a nuclear disaster statistic. I don't want you to, either—now or in the future."

"But you never seemed afraid or concerned about the Niconda plant before. I never was afraid of it. You never said anything but good things about it. You thought nuclear power was the coming thing, the power source that would save our country from its energy problems."

His dad looked at him. "Ned, it just never came home to me like this before. I read some about nuclear power—and it seemed to be a good thing for our country. Yes, newspaper and magazine articles did mention some possible dangers or concerns, but scientists and engineers seemed to be on top of things, to know what they were doing. I had faith that they could solve those problems and assure the safety of nuclear power for us."

"That's what everyone in this town seemed to believe, too, Dad. They wanted to believe that—except for Mr. Abinson."

"And now that I got appointed to this nuclear committee with its responsibilities, I've just begun to realize how ignorant I am about nuclear power. I also don't know how much information I can get from this Senator. So, last night, I wrote some letters to different groups around the country—

some nuclear groups, some antinuclear groups. I have to learn—and learn soon."

It was almost like his dad was talking to himself, rather than answering Ned's questions.

"What gets me really angry about this whole situation, Ned, is how did we get into this? All the statistics by the authorities and scientists, all the benefits I read about nuclear energy and nuclear plants, said they were safe—secure—with it being extremely unlikely that anything serious could happen. So, I worked to build that Niconda plant. I encouraged taxpayers to vote to spend millions of dollars to have that plant near our town—so it could threaten our lives like this. Now, with whatever is going on at that plant—with whatever they decide to do about us here—I feel like I'm not even in control over what other people can do to my life, to my family, to my future. It's incredible!"

"I think I'm beginning to understand, Dad."

24

During the next two days, the news media—especially the TV news—played up the nuclear threat at Niconda. They had experts predict what could happen if the gases continued to escape—or increased—or if the cooling system failed and a melt-down occurred. Constant comparisons were made to the Three Mile Island accident. People in the Three Mile Island area were interviewed about their feelings and thoughts for the people in Wilkenton.

Dad flipped off the TV news in disgust. "All the sensationalism—all the hysteria. What kind of facts does the news actually tell us? They're playing with this crisis, using us and it to build their TV news ratings." Then, he stomped from the living room into his study, shut the door and began typing.

Late in the morning of the fourth day, the bullhorn trucks rolled through the streets again. The bullhorn's voice seemed deafening after the long periods of street silence.

"The emergency has ended. Please, listen to your televisions or radios for further details. . . . The emergency has ended. . . ."

Ned rushed to turn on the TV set.

". . . Scientists and nuclear plant officials report that they have successfully sealed the leak which was permitting radioactive gases to enter into the atmosphere. The cooling system has been repaired enough to allow the scientists to cool down the core and to bring the reactor to a cold shut-down. Clean-up of the dirty water inside the containment building will begin as soon as officials assess the extent of any damage to the plant. The plant will be closed until officials from the Nuclear Regulatory Committee conduct a complete safety inspection and investigation into this accident."

Ned could see the relief on the local newsman's face. It was the first time in four days that he had a pleasant expression—smiled—while reporting about the nuclear plant.

Dad came into the room.

The newsman continued. "Scientists feel that the levels of radiation detected in the atmosphere do not pose an immediate or even long-range threat to the welfare of pregnant women and their unborn children, or to young children. Therefore, the National Guard trucks will begin to transport the women and children back to Wilkenton sometime later today. . . .

"Due to the panic-buying of food and to the restrictions placed on the Wilkenton area during the nuclear danger, food supplies have been sharply reduced in local stores. Emergency supplies will be brought in by the Red Cross. It will take two to three days to replenish . . ."

Later in the evening, Ned and his dad drove to the parking lot. They waited there with all the others, listening for the heavy rumble of trucks.

The sound came echoing through the twilight.

The canvas-topped trucks drove in a single line down the Wilkenton streets to the town meeting place.

When they stopped, Guardsmen jumped out and pulled the rear canvas flaps back. Women and children leaned out waving.

"There they are! There's George's gorilla hanging out," Ned yelled.

George had a big grin on his face as he passed his prized gorilla and a soggy chocolate chip cookie down to Ned. Then George leaped into his dad's arms. Dad put him down and helped his mom from the truck. They hugged and kissed each other for a while—just to help realize that they were all together again.

Back home, after an hour or so of hearing about life in the gym, Ned excused himself. He walked to the phone to call Kathy.

The phone rang on the other end once—twice—three times. No one answered. Five—six times. Ned's hand holding the receiver began to sweat. Finally, on the seventh ring, someone answered.

He heard Kathy's voice say, "Hello?"

"Kath? How are you?"

"OK—I guess." She sounded very tired.

"Is your dad home?"

Kathy didn't answer immediately. "He's—he's home, but he doesn't feel too well. Stomach problems again. He got home two hours ago, and went right to bed. We hardly

152

talked together—even though he's been gone all this time. He just went straight to bed. We don't know what's wrong with him, Ned. But there is something. He looks so pale— and wouldn't eat—just drank glasses and glasses of water. He laughed and said that being cooped up in that plant all this time gave him an upset stomach—no home-cooking. . . . He's trying to fool us."

"Sounds like he should see a doctor—and not just one out at the plant."

"Dad doesn't want to, and Mom doesn't know what to do. I want him to go see our doctor in town, but he's stubborn. Maybe he's afraid—I don't know—But I'm going to see that he goes to a doctor."

"Kathy, did he tell you—well, did he say anything about what happened out there—at the plant? What went on?"

"He wouldn't say anything, Ned—not anything. It's almost as if he didn't want us to know."

25

Special delivery mail that morning had brought a packet of material from the NRC about nuclear plants.

Then Washington, D.C.—the Senator—had called to speak with his dad for over an hour.

When his dad finished talking to the Senator, he looked drained—exhausted. Without saying a word, he took the packet of material and walked into his study, shutting the door behind him. He hung out his "Do Not Disturb" sign and spent the next three hours in there.

Finally, when his dad came out from his study, he looked even more tired, with heavy shadows under his eyes.

Ned and his mom watched him, waiting for Dad to tell them what the Senator had said and what was in that packet of material.

They all went into the kitchen where Dad poured himself a cup of black coffee. With the cup in his hand, he turned and leaned his back against the counter.

"For three hours, I've read the material they sent me—

and I still don't think I have the information I need, or the understanding of this whole nuclear power issue, to conduct any sort of local investigation. According to the NRC, there have been several 'incidents,' not 'accidents,' over the past twenty years in nuclear plants. The majority have been caused or compounded by human error, not mechanical. They feel the structure of the plant and the various backup safety systems have been adequate and improving over the years. No serious damage or injuries have occurred. The future looks bright for nuclear power."

Dad drank the last bit of coffee in his cup and placed the cup on the counter.

"Is that all, Jack?"

"Well, there were some facts and figures about costs, and energy savings—and other things. You know, I have the feeling that what they sent was just a lot of publicity—PR material, rather than an objective look at the past history of nuclear power. So that just means that I'll have to get on my research horse and go out to do a little digging into the history of our plant out there and its family."

"But what did the Senator say to you, Dad?"

"Oh. Him. Well, some experts in nuclear energy and scientists will be flown here to investigate and report on the technical aspects of this accident—excuse me, I should say 'incident'—and I'm to form that citizens' committee immediately now to gather information, interview plant officials and workers and, in general, explain to the people what happened during this crisis. I need to find at least five other people from this area, not involved with working at the plant, to be on this committee with me. I think the Senator said to find people from 'all walks of life.' That may not be so easy. But the Senator instructed me that 'it would be good politics.' "

"Politics! Dad, you mean we all could have gotten killed or received all that radiation junk, and he's worried about politics!"

"Ned, everything is politics, and politics is in everything. There's no getting away from it. I'm sure, for instance, that the Senator would like our committee to whitewash this whole thing—so there won't be any stain on the bright future of his nuclear power. But let me tell you, son, I'm *going* to investigate—and so will this committee. We're going to know what happened out there and why it happened to us." Dad pounded his fist on the table for emphasis. Then he stood up and went upstairs to change clothes.

A half hour later he left the house to search for members to be on his investigation committee.

Ned sat quietly, watching him pass through the kitchen and out to the garage. The car started, the garage door opened, and the car backed down the driveway into the street.

Ned got up and went in search of his mom. He had to get out of the house. He felt caged.

"You need anything, Mom?"

She was washing the bathroom floor. "Let's see." She stopped the mop. "We could use some milk for George and some bread, too. I doubt the grocery stores will have them, though."

"I could meet the Red Cross supply trucks. They'd probably have stuff like milk and bread."

"Probably, they would—but it might be powdered milk. I don't know if George would like that, but we can try." She went back to mopping the floor.

Ned went down the stairs, and left the house.

It was still very quiet in the streets. Some cars did pass by, but very few people were actually outside—walking, working, or playing. Few wanted to risk testing the fresh air.

In the middle of Main Street, just in front of the drug store, stood three large army trucks with Red Cross insignias on each one.

As Ned walked closer, he could see large-lettered lists on the outside of each truck listing what the truck had inside.

Lines of people had already begun forming alongside each truck. The people on line talked in low voices together.

Ned moved to the line for the truck with milk in it. He'd have to go to another line for bread.

Ned stood in back of Mr. Robinson and Mrs. Simons. They turned and nodded to him, smiling, then turned to face front.

Ned overheard Mr. Robinson tell Mrs. Simons, "I've never been so frightened in all my life as I was these past days. That's like an atomic bomb out there. If it blows up, we all go. It's like ten atomic bombs. Some say it could wipe out an area one-quarter the size of a state like Pennsylvania. Imagine!"

Mrs. Simons nodded. "Me, too. I was dizzy I was so scared. How could they build such a thing here? Who needs it if it's that dangerous?"

"Everyone's afraid. Not just here in Wilkenton, but every-where, Mrs. Simons. Have you been watching the national news? We're even mentioned on that. Some of them came here to film the plant—they're here now. We're big news—because we almost got killed by that thing."

Ned glanced around, trying to see cameras, lights, TV news people. Sure enough. They were there setting up their equipment on a truck a hundred yards to the left. They were obviously going to film the people of Wilkenton lined up to receive charity food supplies from the Red Cross. For the next half hour or so, Ned became engrossed with watching the TV group set the stage for their Wilkenton near nuclear disaster coverage. He mechanically moved forward when the line did, but tuned out most of the conversation around him.

When he reached the truck, he could see crates and crates of canned milk inside.

An elderly, gray-haired man sat inside the truck recording names and numbers of cans of milk. A National Guardsman pulled crates and cases to the back opening of the truck, and passed out the cans.

"How many, son?"

Ned looked at the elderly man.

"How many cans do you need?"

Ned hesitated. "I don't know. There's four of us—one a small child, my brother—"

"Give him three cans, Henry." The National Guardsman passed down three cans of milk.

For a moment, when Ned took the cans from him and looked up into his face, he thought it was one of the same Guardsmen who had yelled at him at the grocery store. But, if it was, the man didn't recognize Ned.

Ned moved over to a second truck's line. It was shorter—just for bread.

Someone tapped him on the shoulder.

Ned turned around to see Jake, grinning as always.

"Let me tell you, son. When I say that siren will blow itself again, that siren *will* blow itself again! That's the power of positive thinking!"

Ned had to smile. It was great to hear Jake bantering in the same old way. It broke through this whole business, brought things back to close to normal.

"What are you doing on this line, Jake? This isn't the kind of bread you usually go after."

"Ned-boy, even I get hungry for the real stuff some times. But, you gotta admit, this was one exciting time—full of suspense. Would we all live? Or would we all glow to our end? That was the question, and still is the question." Jake's body couldn't stop bouncing this way and that with his words. Jake could never sit still, and standing on line drove him nuts.

Jake kept up his nonstop chatter until Ned reached the front of the line.

When he peered into the dark truck, he saw her—Jane. Her red hair seemed to glow in the darkness of the truck's interior. She brought some loaves of bread toward him.

She saw him there.

"Hi, Ned. How are you?"

He nodded his head, "OK."

She turned to someone else in the back of the truck. "I'm taking a short break. Be back in a minute." Jane hopped down from the truck.

Ned wished she hadn't—especially with Jake right there.

"You made it through this thing OK? I mean—as far as you know?"

Ned nodded again, but he didn't need those last words "as far as you know."

"Your family all right, too? I thought about you a lot. Hoped you were doing all right."

He didn't really want to talk now, but he couldn't just stand there and not answer her. "Thanks. We're doing fine. My—uh—mom and young brother, you know, they were over there in the Specter Creek school gym with the Red Cross for those few days."

She touched his arm. "That must have been a little scary—I mean not knowing what was going on—and then your mom and brother going away like that?"

Ned nodded.

She went back to the truck and handed him a loaf of bread.

He gripped the bread too hard. "Well, I've got to get back and help out at home. . . ."

She smiled. "I have to get back to work, too. See you again, Ned. Hope you're around to save me on my next march."

Ned couldn't help smiling back at her.

Jane climbed back on the truck and disappeared inside.

When Ned turned to leave, he came face to face with Jake. Jake hadn't lost his grin—and he hadn't missed hearing and seeing everything.

26

The TV national news, newspapers, even discussion and interviews on radio focused on and played up the accident at Niconda and its possible consequences for the people of Wilkenton. Had the people been contaminated? Who could tell?

One health official stated on TV that no direct injuries had been reported by plant officials or by local officials. However, Ned had heard him take a deep breath, and then go on to state that those contaminated by radiation might not have any noticeable injuries or illness for up to fifty years after the contamination.

Ned couldn't imagine waiting fifty years—and not knowing if the radiation was eating away at you or slowly killing you.

NBC interviewed Mr. Ralph Jackson, Director of Public Relations for Niconda.

Ned listened intently, watching the black-suited stocky man as he sat in one of those molded plastic TV chairs. He had the habit of constantly running one hand over his silver-gray hair, patting down the thin hairs on top of his head.

The interviewer posed serious questions to Mr. Jackson about the accident, the safety of the Niconda plant, and the future of nuclear power.

Through the entire interview, no matter how serious the question, Mr. Jackson never stopped smiling.

"Let me explain to you and to the people watching that there was an incident at Niconda. It certainly was not as serious as most people seem to believe. The sirens, staying at home, and other precautions were just safety measures. We feel very conscious of protecting the public's welfare. We were taking no chances at all—none. Let me assure you of that.

"In a way, this incident was good for us. It showed once again that we can prevent an incident from becoming more serious, that our technology and nuclear personnel have the expertise to deal with any situation that might occur at the plant. The way we controlled this situation proved that. It should reassure the public . . ."

Somehow, Ned was *not* reassured.

The front page of the newspaper gave an account of the accident itself and about the investigation that would look into the conditions of the accident. It noted that the NRC would probably spend the next several weeks or so collecting information, before opening its investigation to the public and allowing the public to question them.

Ned read the story of the accident first. It told in more detail about the pipe that had broken so close to the reactor that no valve could cut off the water or redirect the water flowing to cool the core. The position of the break was even out of view of the various video cameras set around the containment building.

Added to this problem was a defective vent on the top of the containment building. Once opened to release small quantities of gaseous wastes—Krypton gas, iodine, and Strontium-90 among others—the vent would not close completely. Various adjustments from the control room only succeeded in jamming the vent into a more open position. At one point, said the experts, the radiation level at the roof of the containment building had jumped to a reading of 450 rads, deadly to any person who entered the area.

Since this was a fission reactor, not a breeder reactor, there was no danger of the core exploding. Only if the steam pressure inside the containment building had built up and then mixed with some explosive gas such as hydrogen might there have been an explosion. By pumping the water through the pipes, Niconda experts and scientists had kept the core cool and brought it to the shut-down. This avoided the "China Syndrome."

Ned broke into a cold sweat as he read the account slowly and carefully. He gritted his teeth at some of the comments by plant officials who played down the potential disaster as just "one-of-those-things" that will happen in a nuclear plant.

"Some 'incident'!" Ned said out loud.

Mr. Jackson was even quoted in the paper as saying that "We welcome the local citizens' committee's questions and examination of this incident at Niconda. We feel that the committee's findings will only serve to reassure the people and build their confidence in nuclear power as the future energy source for our nation."

Ned wanted to talk with his dad about all this, but his dad was too busy organizing the committee and reading piles of materials sent by the government, Niconda, and other agencies around the country.

Instead, he went upstairs to his room. He shut the door so he could be alone—to think.

His eyes wandered over the bookshelves and books in his room. On the floor, in front of the lower shelf, were the books Mr. Abinson had handed him.

Ned walked over, bent down and picked up one of them. The jacket copy began:

"This is the documented, true account of what happened on the afternoon of October 5, 1966, when the control panel inside the Enrico Fermi atomic reactor near Detroit, Michigan, suddenly registered high radiation levels, a sign of critical danger. . . ."

Hesitantly, he opened to the first page of text and, in a few minutes became absorbed in the account of another nuclear accident.

What he read made him dizzy. He had difficulty swallowing, his throat seemed dry. He couldn't believe it.

When this accident happened at the Fermi reactor in Lagoona Beach on Lake Erie, the only emergency plan that officials had in case of a major nuclear accident was to evacuate the area—and that included the cities of Detroit and Toledo, over four million people. Even Ned knew there was no way they could evacuate four million people in a few hours. So, when the accident did occur, officials decided *not* to notify the public.

Gee! thought Ned. How could they just let the people sit there in the middle of that thing and not tell them?

And here it says that in just 1974–75 nearly half of the fifty nuclear reactors in the country had to each be shut down and checked twice within six months to see if there were cracks in the cooling system pipes. Twice in a six-month period! Did they check Niconda, or was that one of the ones they missed? How easy it must be to miss a tiny crack like that, and—man!—what that crack could do!

Some pages from a magazine article dropped out of the book. Ned picked them up. The article told about the past history of nuclear power plants in the United States. An experimental reactor in Idaho Falls, Idaho, in 1961, had exploded, killing three men who were inside the containment building. They died from the intense heat and radiation exposure, but investigators could never determine why this deadly accident had occurred.

A plant near Denver somehow had radioactive helium escape from the chimneys. The radiation over the plant was thirty times normal for a while, and some workers became ill. In Massachusetts, the broken gauges in one plant had caused the containment area to flood with radioactive water several times. A technician in Tennessee at a nuclear plant used a candle to search for air leaks in the pipes. He accidentally started a fire and burned the reactor controls. It took ten hours of frantic rewiring to keep the core from a melt-down. Another nuclear plant in the state of Washington accidentally dumped 60,000 gallons of radioactive water into the Columbia River. How come he'd never heard about that? Then, of course, there was the partial melt-down in the Fermi reactor due to a jammed cooling system.

Ned put the book and article down. He breathed deeply. His stomach churned inside him.

They've got to be joking about all this, he thought. It reads like some crazy science fiction book—but the dates are all here!

He picked up the book and read a paragraph Mr. Abinson had marked. It said that, according to a 1965 Planning Research Corporation report, there would be about a one-in-500 chance for a nuclear accident or catastrophe to occur. But, Ned thought, if the U.S. planned to have over 500 reactors in operation by 1985, would that mean there would be one nuclear catastrophe every year in this country?

After reading books and magazine articles like this, Ned could see why Mr. Abinson had to march—had to express his concerns and fears about what might happen with these nuclear plants.

If people knew about these facts, about these dangers, why then weren't more people marching, speaking out, doing something to make their lives safe? Were they scared—confused—lazy—that uncaring?

Ned closed the book. It was too heavy to read. He had read too much. The pages felt like lead.

27

Two days had passed. Ned hadn't seen Kathy since the afternoon at the grocery store. He wanted to see her—to be with her—but he hesitated just going over to her house. He didn't know how her father was—what her mother would say or do—what he himself would say or do. Since this accident—with the sirens, with staying in the house isolated, his mother and brother taken away—Ned wasn't sure of anything. He wanted to talk with Kathy.

He had tried to call her three—four—five times each day, but either no one answered the phone, or else Kathy's mother answered it, speaking in a strange, distracted voice. She would say that Kathy had the flu or something like that—that she couldn't come to the phone or have visitors.

Ned desperately wanted to be with Kathy, to discuss what he had read with her—but she seemed locked away from him. He had even thought of writing her a letter, but laughed at that idea. He couldn't possibly put down all his thoughts, his feelings for her and about what had happened in a letter. Instead, he sent her a funny "get well" card with pink elephants on the front.

For the first time in two days, Ned's dad ate dinner with them. He looked worn out.

"Hummmmm." His dad cleared his throat to get their attention. "I've been doing a lot of reading and thinking about what has happened to us—to our town—and what still could happen here any time. I feel that I must come out—publicly—in opposition to keeping the Niconda plant open unless they can assure us that it is totally safe for the people's health and welfare.

"I'm not sure—even with what happened—just how popular my voice will be. It might cause some trouble for us . . . I don't know. It might—but I don't see any choice. I can't stand by and watch this happen again."

His mom didn't say anything. She just placed her hand on his arm and squeezed tightly.

Ned nodded in agreement with his dad's words, but also said nothing.

A few seconds of silence passed.

His dad got up from his chair and walked back into his study.

Ned watched the study door close. He listened to the movements inside his dad's room.

Finally, Ned walked from the kitchen to the study door and knocked softly. There was no answer. He knocked again more loudly, more urgently.

"Come on in. It's open."

Ned opened the door slowly. He saw that his dad was sitting with his back to the door.

168

As he entered the room, his dad rotated his swivel desk chair around to face him.

"Oh. Hi, Ned. What's the problem?"

Usually, Dad would take a few minutes just to chat if Ned or Mom came in, but, now, Ned knew that if he didn't have a problem, he shouldn't be here.

"Dad—"

His dad waited for whatever Ned wanted to say.

"Dad, I've been doing some reading—some reading about nuclear plants and things—from a book Mr. Abinson gave me. . . . It's scary, you know?"

Taking off his glasses, his dad gently massaged his eyes. He dropped the hand with the glasses to his lap. He looked directly at his oldest son. "Yes, I know, Ned. The more I read and find out, the scarier this whole thing becomes for me, too."

"But what this book says about radiation and what it can do to you. I mean like receiving just a 100 rems will make you sick—and 300 to 450 will do some real damage to your body—and from 450 to 600 will kill you. You get nauseous, feel weak—and all the time the radiation is destroying your red and white blood cells. I mean—well—Kathy's dad is home sick now. Is he dying? Do I tell Kathy or her mom about all this?"

"He's seen the doctors at the plant, hasn't he?"

Ned nodded his head in reply. "Kathy said he had—and they checked him over. But maybe he needs to see someone else—not in the plant . . . That's some awful way to die."

His dad didn't answer right away. "I think he should see another doctor, but—well—I'm not so sure I'd go telling

Kathy or her mother all this. That might not be the best thing for them. Let a doctor tell them—if he has to. You don't know what her father has—or how bad it is."

"And that gas, Dad, do you know if it really contaminated the air? It can shoot out all sorts of things like strontium and iodine and cesium. Do you know that if a one-year-old breathes Iodine-131, he's three times more likely to have some bad damage done to his body than an adult would who breathed the same stuff? I'm sure glad they got George out of here! But is it still around—still in the air where he can breathe it?"

"Slow down, Ned—slow down. I realize you're worried and full of questions about these things, but I just don't have all the answers yet. I can only tell you that health officials state that they don't detect anything in the air and they were supposed to have checked out the local dairy cows for any contamination. Some traces have been found, and the contaminated milk has been confiscated."

"Then, it *was* in the air."

"Some—I guess."

"And the men who got killed in Idaho Falls—did you know about them, too?"

"I—uh—I just learned about that. The information I've received from government sources doesn't mention any deaths or serious accidents. They even state in one of their reports that major accidents are highly improbable. Those were the words they used 'highly improbable.' I did receive additional information from other nongovernment organizations. And that's where I learned about the serious accidents."

"Dad could—could all these things really be happening—and people—people like us—be so unaware? . . . Do people want these nuclear plants that badly?"

"Those plants are private businesses, Ned. They may be supported by government loans and government insurance, and by our taxes, but they are owned and operated for profit as private businesses.

"The people who lived around Wilkenton before the plant came—mostly farmers and cattlemen—protested the building of the plant. They didn't want it, and worried about what it might do to the environment. But with the huge sums of money backing the plant, with the politics of the electric companies who said we needed this power, and with the overruling force of the federal government, the power plant went through. They all said that Wilkenton was 'the best location.' "

"But, Dad, if they threaten us—endanger our lives—don't we have anything to say about these nuclear plants, anything at all?"

28

Ned saw Mr. Jackson, the Director of Public Relations for Niconda, twice the night before his dad's committee was to begin its collecting of information and interviewing people about the Niconda accident. The first time he came to the Turner home.

At 7:30 Mr. Jackson knocked on the front door.

Dad hadn't expected a visitor.

With barely a "hello" to Ned and his mom, Mr. Jackson disappeared with Dad into the study and closed the study door.

Nearly an hour later, the study door opened and Mr. Jackson walked out, followed by Dad.

"So, Representative Turner, we welcome your committee's investigation and questions, as I have said. I am sure you will give the Niconda plant a clean bill of health and restore public confidence. We will supply our records to your group and will be glad to answer any further questions. Just contact me and let me know how I might help." He reached out to shake Dad's hand.

Dad took Mr. Jackson's hand with little enthusiasm. "Your cooperation will be appreciated, Mr. Jackson. As I mentioned, we would like to question some of your employees at our sessions."

Mr. Jackson's hand dropped to his side. "Well, that remains to be seen. Certainly, anyone who wishes to speak with you may do so. You understand, though, that we cannot and will not order anyone to appear before your committee, and your public relations group, of course, does not have the legal power to bring them in for questioning."

Dad nodded, carefully watching Mr. Jackson's eyes, rather than his smile. "But, Mr. Jackson, our group still represents—or will represent—hopefully, the major public opinion in this area. If the public feels Niconda is a continuing threat to its health and welfare, then I—and my committee—will do all we can to see that the public's health and welfare is protected."

"A very nice speech, Representative Turner. Good politics."

Ned could tell that Dad didn't like or trust this man.

Mr. Jackson left.

Dad stood at the doorway, regarding Mr. Jackson's stiff, fast stride as he moved toward his car.

"That man, Ned, will be trouble for us. He has no intention of allowing his people to testify, or allowing us to threaten the continued operation of that plant in any way."

"What will he do, Dad?"

"I don't know what he'll do. It depends on how much of a threat, how much public pressure, the committee I head seems to have. The people on that committee are workers, farmers, businessmen, and housewives. I just don't know how much influence we'll have."

The second time Ned saw Mr. Jackson was on TV that night.

Niconda had a public service message for the Wilkenton people and Mr. Jackson had the lead role.

"Nuclear power, my friends, is our future. It's the future of our town of Wilkenton—and of this great nation we call the United States of America. Nuclear energy is a wonder of modern engineering, science, and technology blended for the betterment of mankind.

"Nuclear energy will provide cheap, efficient power. It has proven to be safe and plentiful. With our careful control, it has and will continue to be much better for our environment than any other effective alternative source of energy. . . . And, most of all, nuclear power gives us independence—our freedom from reliance on foreign governments to supply us with essential energy sources such as oil.

"Truly, nuclear energy is the future for us—and for our children."

"The future!" Ned said out loud, though no one else was in the room. "That guy's got to be joking! What future—if there's a bad accident and you have all that junk in the air you're breathing, in the food you're eating, and inside your body? It might be twenty years or more before I could tell what this stuff is doing to *my* future. You, Mr. Jackson, won't be around. You'll probably be long dead before then. But I will be around—and I'll get the results of what your plant does to me. Some public service!"

174

29

School had started. Still, Ned had not seen Kathy. She hadn't come to school.

He had called her at home—but without luck. Either there was no answer or there was a busy signal.

Finally, Ned couldn't stand it any longer. Seeing her was more important—much more important—than worrying about what might happen when he did see her. He cut his last two classes and went over to her house.

The shades were drawn down over all the windows. The house seemed dark and silent.

Ned went to press the doorbell, but a paper sign taped over the bell said, "Please do not ring."

He knocked softly on the hardwood door. He waited, then knocked again. He couldn't hear a sound, any movement from inside the house.

Leaving the front door, he walked slowly around the house until he came to the kitchen door in back. Through the glass window, he could see Kathy, dressed in a blouse

175

and jeans, sitting at the kitchen table drinking from a cup.

He rapped lightly on the glass window of the door.

She looked up, startled.

Ned smiled.

Hesitatingly, Kathy pushed back the chair and stood up. She gave a concerned look toward the living room doorway, and then moved quickly to the kitchen door. Unlocking and opening it, she motioned Ned to come in.

Ned took her in his arms and hugged her tightly.

Kathy leaned her head against his shoulder and sobbed softly.

Carefully, silently closing the door, she drew him over to a corner of the kitchen.

"Oh, Ned!" she whispered. "I've missed you. I needed you."

Ned held her more tightly.

"My mother—my father—"

Ned pushed himself slightly away from her, so he could look at her face. "What's the matter, Kath? What about your folks?"

She laid her head on his shoulder. "My father came home from the plant after the accident was over—and he was sick. Really sick, Ned. Pale and vomiting and weak. The doctors said—they said— he had too much radiation exposure. They said he'd probably be all right . . . if he didn't get any more radiation for a while—"

Ned sensed the fear, the desperate concern, she had for her father.

"And my mother—Oh, I don't know—my mother has sort of gone all to pieces. Since my father came home, she hasn't left the house. She hardly leaves his side, even when he's sleeping. She's called in every day sick to work. She intercepts every phone call, and at the same time, dreads answering the phone. She sits by his side in a chair, hardly speaking at all. She just sits there staring at him, her face tense and drained. Even my father's tried cheering her up. She's—she's just so worried—so worried—"

"And you, Kath? Why couldn't I see you—speak with you? Why didn't you come to school today?"

"I was just so down—so depressed, Ned, that I didn't want to talk—to see anyone. I just wanted us to survive as a family. I wanted my father to be well. And, then, I just couldn't leave my mother and father. She is barely functioning, barely doing anything. I couldn't just leave her at home with my father like that. So, I stayed here and took care of them—both of them."

"But it can't go on like this, Kath. You all can't stay locked up in the house, with the shades down and everything."

She nodded. "I know, Ned. I'm hoping that she'll be OK soon. . . . And the shades are down because the light hurts my father's eyes."

A weak whisper came into the kitchen. "Kathy . . . Kathy . . ."

Kathy froze and listened. "That's my father. He's been sleeping in the living room during the day. I'll go see what it is."

She walked through the doorway to the living room and disappeared from Ned's sight.

A few moments later, she returned to him. "He knows you're here—and wants you to come in. OK?"

"Sure."

Kathy's father lay on the couch covered with two blankets, even though the day was warm. Under his head was a large bedroom pillow.

He didn't speak to Ned—just lifted his hand slightly.

"How are you, Mr. Jenkins?"

"A little better," he whispered. His voice sounded dry and lifeless.

"Mother's asleep upstairs," Kathy said.

Ned stood there awkwardly for several silent moments. Then he finally asked, "What happened?"

Kathy looked at Ned with a startled expression. She shook her head, to try and tell him not to ask.

"Water—contaminated, radioactive water—spilled in reactor floor area. Needed to clean it up fast," said the low whisper. "Too long in there—too long."

"Didn't you have a protective suit or something like that?"

"Too high." Her father stopped his whisper to shake his head. "Had masks and suits—still can stay in there for only seconds—one minute at a time. Suits won't protect when radiation is that high—won't—" The voice stopped. Her father seemed exhausted from his effort to explain.

Kathy looked from her father to Ned. "They said he received something like 280 rems at the plant. You're not supposed to be exposed to anywhere near that much in a year—that's the safety measure. Some others wouldn't go in there to clean up the water. My father volunteered. . . . They don't know what the exposure will do to him yet. They don't think it will hurt him permanently if he stays away from receiving more exposure. But they don't really know for sure."

She seemed to be asking Ned a question, rather than telling him what had happened. He wanted to answer her, to say, "Don't worry. Your father will not receive any more radiation—and he won't be harmed by this." But, of course, he couldn't.

Her father's voice broke through again. "There's a lot—a lot that goes on in there—in the plant, Ned. The public will never know about what goes on." Her father's voice increased in its intensity and pitch.

"What do you mean, Mr. Jenkins?"

Her father waved his hand in the air. "Lots of things— little things—that could become big things maybe. Who knows?"

Ned knelt down beside Mr. Jenkins so he could hear him better. "Name some—name one, for example."

"You know the control room? There's supposed to be someone in there all the time. But this one time, one of the two supervisors in the control room took a break, and the other one, a few minutes later, got this stomach cramp— well, they both—*both* of them—were out of the control room—for five minutes they were out . . ." His head dropped back on the pillow.

"And, Ned, that's only one of the human weaknesses— errors—at Niconda. That doesn't include a broken gauge, a pipe leaking. One time there was a damaged control rod . . . people don't know." His voice trailed off.

Ned turned to Kathy. "Was your father the only one to get exposed to the contaminated water?"

"No. He said that some other men—three, I think—were in there with him—all volunteers to try to stop the leaking valve. But he was the only one to actually slip and fall into the water and receive that heavy dose. It was because his suit was faulty. The plant checked him out. They can't do a lot when you've been exposed—just wait—just wait and make sure he stays away from any further exposure. When he gets better, they'll give him a job elsewhere in the plant."

"Do the other men know what happened to your father, Kath?"

She nodded. "People know. Word travels around town, especially among the plant workers. It was an accident—and he volunteered . . . He was unlucky. I guess—I guess that's what they'd say."

"But these other things—the control room, broken equipment—my dad's committee should hear about these things. They might be able to bring public pressure on the plant—maybe have it closed until it's safe."

Her father's whispered voice said, "No, Ned. I can't talk to any—any—committee."

"Why?"

"Can't, Ned. They'd fire me—they'd fire—"

Ned didn't have a reply. Kathy's father closed his eyes.

Kathy moved back to the kitchen. Ned followed.

"You'd better go now, Ned. My mother may be up any moment—and I—I don't know how she's going to act—or feel about you being here right now."

"Kathy, I—"

"I know, Ned . . . I love you for coming here—and for

caring." She pulled his head down and kissed him.

The kitchen door closed behind him. Ned looked through the window to see Kathy leaning against the doorway, looking toward the living room.

30

That night Ned's dad worked late at his office in town.

Ned and his mom sat at home watching the early evening local news. They heard the broadcaster say:

"On the local scene today, we interviewed State Representative Jack Turner about his new role as head of the citizens' committee on nuclear affairs. We especially wanted to know what his group would do in light of the recent nuclear accident at Niconda.

"Mr. Turner, what do you and your committee plan to tell the people of this area about nuclear safety and Niconda?"

Ned's dad stood straight, pushing his glasses further up the bridge of his nose and facing the TV newsman squarely. "We will try to gather as much information as possible, interview as many people as we can—and then make a report and recommendations about improving the safety of the Niconda Nuclear Plant."

"Do you feel that the plant has been unsafe? Or still is?"

"With the recent accident, the panic and possible dangers

that accident caused, I feel that the safety of nuclear plants should be a primary concern. Don't forget that the people in Pennsylvania had to—and are still—living with the Three Mile Island accident. Our accident never grew quite so serious, and I, for one, want to avoid any more such accidents—potential disasters—in the future."

"But, Mr. Turner, just what powers—just how can your committee do anything about the operations and safety at Niconda?"

"This committee doesn't have any legal powers. It, in itself, cannot subpoena and swear in witnesses, nor order the plant to close down, nor direct safety changes to be made. We can, however, make the public aware of what is happening at the plant and what we feel should be changed to guarantee our safety. We also have the ear of some important Senators in D.C. They're the ones who decided to establish these local citizens' committees in various parts of the country. Hopefully, then, we can bring public pressure—a good deal of public pressure—to bear if necessary."

"Thank you, Representative Turner, for your candid remarks."

His dad sounded great!

The call from the Senator in Washington, D.C., came later that night after his dad had come home. That phone call brought his dad out raging.

"Do you know that man thinks I should soft-pedal this whole thing? He said I'm misusing my appointment as head of the nuclear public relations committee, that I'm supposed to promote nuclear energy and plants, not attack them—not

183

try to shut them down. He said he doesn't want to see me ruin a promising political career by attacking my main political support, the Niconda people. We almost get killed—and he's worried about politics! Can you believe that?"

Dad didn't wait for anyone to answer. He just stalked into his study and slammed the door shut.

Up in his room, Ned read the local Wilkenton paper. He came to an editorial that focused on his dad and the committee.

The editorial stressed the need for nuclear safety and for better ways to improve that safety. But it also noted that no disaster had occurred. The editor praised the officials and the operation of the Niconda plant for the way in which they had prevented a major crisis.

In one section of that editorial, the editor commented on his dad's management of the citizens' committee investigation:

"From his public statements and the direction he has given to his committee, it appears that our local State Representative, Mr. Jack Turner, wants a lengthy investigation of the Niconda plant—and, ultimately, wants to shut down the plant completely. This committee, the longer it maintains its investigation, certainly provides Mr. Turner with a good deal of public exposure and publicity, which he hasn't had before. He wants to incite the public by dwelling on the farfetched, possible horrors of a nuclear accident. It would be better if he would place the great benefits of nuclear power to this community in proper perspective to those imagined dangers. We think Representative Turner, if he is

184

truly representing the people in this area, should reconsider his position."

Dad was certainly taking the heat for this investigation.

. . . and to think that this editor could accuse his dad of grandstanding, of using this committee and this nuclear accident just to boost his own political career. It was just the opposite. Why couldn't that editor see what his dad was trying to do?

Ned crumpled up the paper and flung it to the floor in disgust.

31

Kathy returned to school four days after Ned had visited her at her house.

"He's better, I guess. He sits up now, Ned. The doctors say that it will take some time—but the plant is taking care of everything."

"I'll bet they are. . . . They would take care of *everything*, from what I've seen."

"What's the matter with you?"

"What's the matter? That plant is what's the matter. They're taking care of my dad, too—and the investigation—and nobody seems to care too much, you know?" Ned turned down the hallway and began walking quickly away from her.

Kathy ran to catch up with him.

"Ned? Wait a minute. What's the matter?" She caught his jacket sleeve and tugged at him, so he would stop and turn around.

"Didn't you read the paper? They said my dad is using the

committee to boost his political career. They said that Niconda should be given a clean OK—no problems out there—by the committee. They want the committee to end its investigation. So does the Senator in Washington. Who do you think is behind all this—about stopping my dad? I'll tell you who is—Niconda people! Niconda's 'taking care of everything,' you see?"

"What you're saying may be true, but why yell at me? I love you, Ned. I want to help."

People walked around them as they talked in the middle of the hallway. Ned took Kathy's arm and pulled her over to a secluded corner of the hall.

"You want to help?"

"You know I do, Ned."

"OK, then. Convince your father that he should testify before my dad's committee. His testimony, his description of what goes on out there—the faulty equipment, the people's mistakes—could make the difference. It would show some of the dangers. It would show that my dad is right in keeping this committee going so they can collect enough information to ask that the plant be shut down until it has a very thorough inspection and much better safety measures. Don't you see? You can convince him, Kath. You can."

Kathy stood there breathing deeply. She sighed. "No, Ned. I can't. If he ever testified about things like that or was even seen speaking with your dad—and your dad told about some of those things—they'd fire my father. He wouldn't have a job."

"But he's got to, Kath. What about all the other people around here? What about the people in the state who could be killed or contaminated in a nuclear accident? Don't you care about them? Doesn't he?"

"Of course, I care, Ned Turner. I *do* care—and so does he! But I care more about my own father. There might be another accident—there might not. But if my father speaks to yours, he won't have a job, that's for certain. What's he supposed to do with the rest of his life after that? Sit around like a vegetable until he dies? Who's going to pay our bills? To support us? My mother with her $150 a week bank job? It would kill my father not to be working."

"He could find another job. There are other jobs around. He has an engineering degree—"

She shook her head. "Not for him. He likes nuclear engineering. The only plant for that anywhere near here is Niconda. And do you really think—really think—that someone would hire him anywhere else? Hire a man who betrayed his last employer?"

"Kathy, he has to. It's too important to everyone not to—"

"No, Ned. I know how you feel—about your dad—but no. . . . And closing that plant would also mean people in this town—your friends and neighbors—would not be working. They won't like that, Ned. Think about it."

"I have." He left her standing there.

Ned walked out of the school. There was no way he could sit through classes today.

32

He had spent the entire school day wandering—just wandering across the dry, desolate desert lands, kicking sagebrush. He hadn't even missed not eating lunch.

With what he had read and learned about nuclear power, with what he had seen his dad contend, Ned knew he just couldn't accept that Niconda plant here in Wilkenton. But, if he or his dad really came out strong and said or did something about the plant—like proposing that it close for a long time—well, their friends and the people of the town would lose money, their jobs. The people would hate him and his dad. His dad could end up just like Mr. Abinson—driven out of town. Kathy would leave him because of his dad—and he loved her.

At five, Ned came home. He picked up the newspaper and took it to his bedroom, not stopping to speak to anyone.

Sitting on his bed, he spread the paper out and began turning the pages.

The editorial headline "Political Ploy Must End" caught

his eye. It was another editorial attack in the Wilkenton paper on his dad, but much worse this time than last.

"This investigation committee, sponsored by some Senators back in Washington, and used by Jack Turner, our State Representative, who is supposedly representing our best interests, must stop now. It has continued too long, wasted too much of the public's time and money, another example of federal spending and waste. We have heard of no new or startling information that has come forth from this investigation, other than that there was an incident at Niconda, and everything was quickly brought under control.

"We do, however, have our suspicions about Mr. Turner's motives. If he is supposed to be open-minded in this investigation, if he is to represent the people of this town and their interests, if he is not out to promote a cause, then, why, we ask, was his son seen marching with the protesters in the last demonstration at Niconda? We have witnesses who will swear that Ned Turner, Jack Turner's son, was at the plant during the demonstrations. Ned Turner—it seems, according to these witnesses—even managed to assault two townspeople who had been asked to observe the demonstrations and report the demonstrators' activities back to the city council.

"Should we assume it's a case of like son, like father? Could it be that Ned Turner, a naïve sixteen-year-old, has these strong anti-Niconda feelings, and that his father does not? We could hope so, but we doubt it. Therefore, we call for a public meeting this Saturday morning at the high school gym to determine how the people of Wilkenton truly feel about their nuclear plant. Do they want it open and operating? Or closed? We ask that only those who are residents of the Wilkenton area attend this meeting. Let's find out just whom Mr. Turner does represent."

Ned sat there staring blankly at the newspaper. He couldn't believe it. He couldn't believe they could say such things about him—and about his dad. His dad knew Ned wasn't one of those demonstrators. His dad believed him. He understood.

Ned fell back on his bed, his eyes fixed on the ceiling.

All he could think about was somehow denying what the paper had said. He had to clear himself—defend himself. People in this town—his friends—would probably hate him if they thought he was one of those demonstrators. They'd hate him.

When he did get up from the bed to go downstairs to see his dad, Ned's knees felt weak. He thought his legs would buckle under him at any moment.

He found his dad wasn't home yet. Dinner wasn't ready either.

Instead, Ned went to the TV and turned it on.

For a second, the screen remained blank. Then, there appeared the words, "The following is a paid public service message from the Columbia Electric Company, Inc."

The TV screen showed a panoramic view of the setting sun and the buildings of the Niconda plant. The buildings seemed fresh and almost attractive in the red rays of the desert sun. The camera zoomed in toward an office window of the plant, and then into the office itself where Mr. Jackson sat working behind a long, wood-grained desk. He looked up, nodded and smiled, as the camera zoomed to a tight close-up of him.

"Good evening," he said. "I'm glad you could visit us here at Niconda, your nuclear facility." He got up from his desk and began to walk slowly toward the camera. "We would like to take you on a brief tour of the plant and show you how it operates."

For the next five minutes, the TV viewers were led to the various parts of the Niconda plant—the reactor and containment building, waste treatment plant, cooling tower, control room, intake structure, administrative offices, and even the recreational area for plant personnel. Special emphasis was placed on how safe the plant was with all its various backup systems. The workers all seemed to be cheerful and to be enjoying their work.

After the tour, Mr. Jackson sat on the edge of his desk in a casual attitude. He spoke in friendly tones to the viewers. "Very simply, without this plant here, many of us would be out of work, schools could not open because of the lack of tax money paid by the plant, roads would not be repaired or built—the very town of Wilkenton would not be prospering as it now is, if it would even exist at all." The screen flashed black-and-white pictures of people out of work, waiting on bread lines, of closed schools, broken roads, darkened buildings.

"Our technology is constantly improving, as is our knowledge about how to use nuclear power more effectively and with less cost to our customers. But the choice is up to you, my friends and neighbors. You can recommend that we close this plant down, or you can recommend that we stay open to employ the people of this town and to serve the people of this town and state."

Ned turned off the TV.

He sat in the overstuffed chair—angry. He was angry at the Niconda ad—angry about the attacks on his dad, angry at the position he suddenly found himself in.

His dad missed dinner again. Ned hardly spoke during the meal. His mother remained silent, lost in her own thoughts, almost unaware that Ned was there. Although she did support his dad's stand, she had become increasingly worried about what might happen to his dad, to them as a family. Only George kept chattering on and on.

After dinner, Ned went up to his room, shut the door, and stayed there until close to nine.

Ned heard the car pull up in the driveway, the garage door open and close, and the front door open. Dad was home.

Ned waited for a few minutes. Then he went down to talk with his dad.

The house was quiet. Both George and his mom had gone to sleep.

Ned knocked on the closed study door.

His dad opened it. Dad was worn out. His tie swung loosely from his neck and open-collared shirt. His hair was tousled and the gold-rimmed glasses balanced dangerously on the tip of his nose.

"How's it going, Dad?" Ned said in a very low, subdued voice.

Dad turned around and walked back to his desk chair. He

sat down heavily. "Not good, Ned. Not too good at all. Just had one member of the committee quit because she was afraid of what people might think of her if we convinced the government to close the plant. She said she couldn't handle the pressures any more. Another member said he would quit next week if we didn't wind this thing up."

Ned nodded. "Things changed pretty quickly, didn't they? People don't seem to be too interested in what happened to cause that accident."

"You're right there, son. The first reaction after that near disaster we had was that almost everyone wanted an immediate investigation—wanted the plant closed down. Most didn't want any part of it, didn't want to see the plant open again. Now, after some days have passed and no one can *see* any real damage done by the accident, they just want Niconda closed long enough to do any necessary repairs. They want to make sure they'll have jobs and income. They want everything back to 'normal.' Most of the people can't seem to be bothered looking twenty or thirty years into the future—or considering what might happen to the next generation of people because we didn't take the time and concern to make sure these nuclear plants are really safe now.

"I'd like to see that plant closed until they can guarantee our safety. Otherwise, I'm not willing to pay the price—to take the risk of another accident. Unfortunately, son, I'm now in the minority in this town. Many of the Wilkenton people have started thinking about their new car or boat or vacation or house payments. All of which they wouldn't have or be able to afford if that plant closed down. But how many new cars and boats, how many house payments, make up for possibly a deformed child, for disease, or someone's life?"

"It sounds crazy, Dad—and I—uh—I just wanted to say I am—well—sorry for that thing in the paper about me being a demonstrator. You know I wasn't one of them. You know that—"

His dad smiled and nodded back at him. "I know, Ned. I'm sorry they dragged you into this, but you have to understand that people here look at this citizens' committee as a threat to the Niconda plant and to the survival of the town. That's funny—ironic—isn't it? It's just the opposite of what this committee was supposed to be. People here will do just about anything to make certain we don't succeed. Or, just let's say, I'm not exactly planning on winning a new term as State Representative from Wilkenton."

"Well, I'm sorry, Dad—really. But, Dad, I want to live here. I don't want my friends and everyone to hate me. And I don't want you to get hurt because of me and what the newspaper said. I want to stay here—Kathy, my friends, everything's right here for me."

His dad leaned back in his padded desk chair and looked at Ned. "I know how you feel, son. I truly think I do. It's the same for me. My career, friends, life have been here in Wilkenton—and I like living here. But, Ned, I've made a decision that I feel is important enough to follow through on. It won't be easy for me—especially if I stay here in Wilkenton—but I think it's a necessary decision for me—and for the people of this town."

"But, Dad, I—"

"It's not like the paper says, Ned. It's not 'like father, like son' or the reverse. You have to make your own decisions.

You can even go out there and speak to your friends—to the newspaper if you want—and tell them that you don't believe the plant should be closed, that you don't agree with me. I'll handle that—if it's what you want and need to do. But, Ned, you have to make your own choices, your own decisions, and stick by them."

33

Ned watched his dad dress and prepare for this Saturday morning meeting that would probably end his political career.

Last night and this morning, on both TV and radio, there had been numerous public service messages reminding the people of Wilkenton about the importance of this meeting at the high school gym. Many of these messages were accompanied by other "public service" messages by Mr. Jackson of Niconda. His dad didn't have a chance.

"Dad, do you want me to go to that meeting with you?"

His dad paused in the middle of tying a knot in his necktie. He looked across at his oldest son. "Do you want to be there, Ned?"

"Dad, I—uh—believe—believe in what you're doing. I think you're right and all—but I—um—don't think I want to go."

"I always want you with me, Ned. I want you to understand—and, hopefully, support—what I'm doing. You can come with me if you want, but if you don't, that's OK. I can understand."

Ned shuffled his feet back and forth on the floor. "I don't think so . . . I don't think I can go."

"That's all right, Ned. In some ways, it might be better. I didn't want your mother to come either, although she wants to be there. The less they see you involved with this, the better, probably."

"But, Dad, will you be OK? I mean—well—you'll be pretty much alone in there."

"Thanks, son, but I'll be all right. They'll have TV cameras and newspeople in there taking everything down. So, I think it'll be calm."

Ned didn't say anything.

"Has it been a rough week for you at school, Ned?"

How could he tell his dad? It had been a bad week. During school, he had avoided Kathy because he was still angry with her about not convincing her father to testify. He had walked down the halls alone, leaving her standing behind him. But it hadn't made him feel any better. It just made things more rotten.

He had refused to go out with friends—and would hardly talk to any of them. He thought they would say something about being a demonstrator or about his dad, but they never did. There were one or two kids who did make some cracks about what his dad was doing to this town—but that was all. Except for old Jake who kept shaking his head and saying things like "weird—very strange—you're acting very strange, old Ned."

But the week probably hadn't been anywhere near as bad for him as the week had been for his dad. So, Ned just shook his head—no.

His dad slipped into his sport coat—the checked one—and took his briefcase under his arm. He walked into the kitchen hugged and kissed Mom and George, then he came back out.

"I'll see you around—probably be back sooner than you think." He closed his fist and tapped Ned lightly on the chin. "Hang in there, son."

Dad opened the front door, then the garage door. He backed the car out and left.

Ned's body seemed paralyzed, but his mind swirled.

He couldn't decide whether he should go to the meeting or not. He didn't want to see Kathy or her father and mother there—not there against his own dad. He didn't want to face his friends and neighbors who'd be there—attacking his dad, thinking that his dad was using the town and the accident to further his own career. And that Mr. Jackson—Ned hated him. He hated him for what he was trying to do to his dad. Jackson probably was behind most of the editorials in the Wilkenton paper.

But Ned couldn't erase the picture of his dad alone at that meeting. There were still some committee members on his side, but they wouldn't really make much difference. His dad would have to face Mr. Jackson, knowing that his friends had turned against him. The people there might be angry— very angry.

Ned knew what his dad was trying to do. His dad was

sacrificing his own career to try to save the town—to save the *people* of the town. What was so wrong about that?

Even if his dad had said it was all right if Ned didn't come to the meeting . . . even if he understood his son's reasons for not wanting to attend . . .

34

Cars filled the high school parking lot.

In front of the main entrance to the school marched fifty or sixty demonstrators. They must have come from the Spokane area. Sheriff's deputies kept them back from blocking the entrance to the school gym.

Ned walked toward the door. He stopped to look at the demonstrators carrying their signs against nuclear power and nuclear plants. No one looked familiar.

After entering the building, Ned walked slowly down the long hallway. His footsteps echoed through the deserted hall. The dark green and light green checked floor tile seemed to stretch on endlessly.

Ned neared the gym.

Just outside the door he saw Kathy.

He stopped to look at her. It was as if he were seeing her—seeing them together—for the first time in a long time. Really seeing. What a fool he'd been. He loved her—he needed her. She was worried and frightened for her father and mother, just like he was for his own dad. Instead of helping her, being there when she needed him, he had turned on her. He had walked away from her because she had wanted to protect her father.

Kathy hadn't seen him yet. She stood there listening intently to what was happening inside the gym.

"Kath—Kathy . . . I'm—I'm sorry."

She turned, took his hand in hers, and squeezed it. "Me, too."

"I—I have to go in there, Kath. My dad's in there—alone—and, well, I want to be with him."

She nodded.

"I know how I feel about this nuclear thing, and that plant out there. I know I will stand with my dad, Kath."

She smiled—a tight, tense smile.

"OK, Kath?"

"I'll be here waiting, Ned, when you come out, no matter what. I don't want to go in there, but I'll be here waiting for you."

Ned let go of her hand and walked through the gym doorway.

In one of the back rows, Ned found a seat between a woman in her thirties and a man in his fifties. The man was dressed in slacks and a sweatshirt.

They had placed two long tables at the front of the gym. One had Mr. Jackson behind it, the other his dad.

Mr. Jackson stood up. He walked to the other side of the table.

"My friends, we must make an important decision here today—an important decision for you and for the Niconda Nuclear Plant. As you well know, there was an incident at the Niconda plant. We took all the necessary precautions, and corrected the problem. We did inconvenience the people in this area for a few days, but that was just our concern for your safety. Nuclear plants are safe—as safe as other types of industry that work with delicate materials, if not safer. Aside from the accident at Idaho Falls—and that was an experimental reactor, not one in commercial use—there have been no other serious injuries, much less deaths. What other industry can say that?"

Ned listened as Mr. Jackson, a good speaker, went on and on about the benefits of nuclear power.

The woman next to Ned kept nodding in agreement. "He's right. We need that plant here. Nothing's happened to us. If they shut down that plant, the town's through."

The man on the other side of Ned sat as if frozen, listening intently.

"And so, my neighbors and friends, the choice is yours: Do we keep on with this endless investigation and this committee until they find some way to close down our plant, or do we end this investigation now? You are the people of Wilkenton and this committee supposedly represents your interests. Therefore, you should decide. Thank you." Mr. Jackson went back to his seat.

A stocky, blond-haired man, Mr. Shipley, the moderator of the meeting, said, "Thank you, Mr. Jackson. And now we will hear from State Representative Jack Turner, chairman of the citizens' committee on nuclear energy for this area. Mr. Turner."

His dad stood up and walked to a central area between the two tables.

"Thank you, Mr. Shipley and Mr. Jackson. I would like to

clarify my position. I am *not* against nuclear energy in itself. I am *not* opposed to nuclear power plants. I am, however, opposed to these plants when they threaten the public's health and welfare.

"You must understand that no one can guarantee the safety of these nuclear plants—like Niconda—at least, not now. The potential for a catastrophic accident, killing thousands of people, injuring hundreds of thousands, deforming unborn and young children, ruining hundreds of thousands of acres, hangs over us as long as a nuclear plant operates. Though, as Mr. Jackson notes, there have been no major nuclear accidents yet, many close calls have occurred in nuclear plants across the nation, as well as here. The human factor enters in, and humans make mistakes. Mechanical failures have occurred. It would only take one major accident, one costly error or breakdown, and the results of that accident would be horrendous. Does nuclear energy mean that much to us? Do our jobs mean more than our children's future? Is it worth the risk?

"So, I ask that you give us—this citizens' committee— your full support, so that we may continue to work for your best interests and welfare. Thank you."

A small group of people off in the right corner of the gym applauded. So did a few others scattered through the audience. When Ned applauded, the people on either side of him gave him a strange look and slid to the other sides of their chairs.

Mr. Shipley stood up. "I would now entertain a motion to vote on whether you feel this committee should continue its investigation or not. Yes, Mr. Wiggins?"

The man sitting next to Ned rose to his feet. "I move that we put the issue to a vote, and that we take a standing vote here. I want to see who is with us in this town and who isn't."

Someone in another part of the room seconded the motion.

"OK," said Mr. Shipley. "Now. All those in favor of ending this investigation, please stand up."

The whole audience in the gym seemed to move to its feet.

The woman next to Ned looked down at him. Ned remained seated. "What's the matter with you, boy? Get up. You're old enough to vote on this thing. This is your town."

Ned didn't rise. He looked up at the woman and replied, "I know it is. It's also my future they're voting on."

Men assigned to count the votes walked up and down the rows tabulating the total vote.

"OK. Please be seated. Those in favor of continuing this investigation, rise."

Jack Turner stood up behind his table. The people in the corner stood also, and so did one or two others in the audience. Maybe twenty-five in all. Ned looked around the gym, hoping more would get to their feet.

Ned placed the palms of his hands on the edge of the bleacher. Slowly he pushed himself up and stood straight and tall.

The man next to him glared at him. "What are you doing, boy? Sit down here right now!"

Ned didn't look at the man. "I know what I'm doing. I know. I'm Jack Turner's son—and I'll stand by my dad."

His dad saw him. Their eyes met from across the gym. Jack Turner smiled at his son.

Ned smiled back. He knew that this vote wouldn't stop his dad. Ned Turner walked down the bleacher steps to be with him.